IN PURSUIT OF FRUIT

GRASP GOD'S GRAND GOAL FOR YOUR LIFE

LUCAS KITCHEN

ISBN: 978-1-68543-000-9

Published by Free Grace International WWW.FREEGRACE.IN

Mailing Address: 2 Circle Rd. Longview, TX 75602

Lucas Kitchen (1982-) Lucas.Kitchen@icloud.com

WWW.LUCASKITCHEN.COM

CONTENTS

Dedicated to John.
You garden harder than anyone I know.

PART I
THE GARDENING GOAL

1

WELCOME TO THE JUNGLE

You find yourself in a jungle of sorts. Your feet squish into the floor of this overgrown stretch of wilderness. The sun is shining dappled softly downward. Its amber warmth caresses the side of your face. Green surrounds, but you wonder how many of these plants are poisonous. Thorn-laden vines, weeds, and fungus grow everywhere you look. Where the undergrowth doesn't cover, there are rocks that jut up from the craggy topography. The forest has a violence and aggression that is frightening. It is unkempt and forgotten. None the less it is yours, bought with the property you now own.

I'll put the new garden here, you decide. You dream of possibilities. Will it be a flowerbed, vegetable garden, or even a farm field of rich crops? The ideas are endless. The potential excites you, but that's all it is right now, potential.

"This is where it begins," you say to no one in particular. You reach into your pocket and retrieve a single envelope you bought at the feed store. The kind clerk, who had insisted on being called Aunt Loola, wrote her number across the paper flap.

"Planting a garden?" she had asked.

"Yeah, I thought I'd try," you responded.

"Call me anytime if you have questions?" she had offered as she penned her number across the seed envelope. You nodded politely, knowing you never would.

You pull open the flap of the envelope and upend the paper container. Into your palm falls a handful of seeds. You place all but one back inside. You look down at the tiny sphere, a miniature world of life, dreaming about the majestic mystery locked inside.

You turn your palm downward and let the seed fall, hoping that it can reach the soil. You watch it plummet toward the dark dirt below. The tangled array of thorns and vines will make it nearly impossible for the fruit seed to ever grow to fruition, but the gesture makes you feel a warm sense of accomplishment.

Tumbling to the earth, the seed sticks the landing. With the toe of your shoe, you press the seed gently into the rough soil. You glance once more at the thorns, vines, and rocks that make the wild landscape so untenable. You turn and walk toward your house, not far from the patch of overgrowth. Your garden has begun.

2
YOU THE JUNGLE

The allegory in the previous section is the scene of your Spiritual birth. When you believed in Jesus for eternal salvation, the Holy Spirit placed eternal life in you.[1] It was like a seed-filled with the potential that eternal life presents. Like an infant sapling to-be, accompanied by a dubious crowd of thorns and weeds, your eternal life began.

There is a beautiful, albeit mysterious, story that Jesus told. He laid out the story of a particular garden with various kinds of soil. There was some that was packed down so hard that seed could never grow. There was dirt that had thorns and weeds, and there was rocky ground as well. In the fictitious tale, some seeds don't take root, others are choked, and a precious few bear a crop of fruit. The mysterious story confused his disciples. They asked him about it later when they were in private.

Jesus explained that the seed is the word of God, and the soil is the heart and mindset of the potential believer. Jesus ends the story by explaining that the one with good soil will experience a bountiful harvest. You can read the story in a few of the gospels, but my favorite retelling is in Luke chapter eight.

Jesus' analogy hints at the ultimate goal of the Christian life. I think there is hardly any metaphor that is better at describing our situation as Christians. Would you like to know the ultimate goal of your life? Don't worry; we'll get to that soon enough.

We will revisit this overgrown garden and the single seed throughout this book. Its competitive location is a place that we will return to many times. It illustrates well the things that we must come to understand before we can grasp and accomplish our life's ultimate goal.

3
BATTLE GARDEN

It's been a few days since you planted the fruit seed in the wild patch of woods behind your house. Now, after waiting with impatience, you return once more to the spot where the seed fell. Being careful, you push aside the thorns and vines, looking for the spot where it found the convoluted earth.

To your utter amazement, there is a tiny sprig, barely more than a twig sprouting up from the ground. You gasp in astonishment at the new life. You straighten up, letting the thorns and vines take their place once more. The seed's little sapling is overshadowed by the violent growth that surrounds. You look at everything that is fighting for space.

This is a battlefield. Now you turn your attention to the weeds, thorns, and vines. They want the same thing that the baby fruit tree wants. They want to win. They fight for every inch of sun and soil. They are in direct competition with the fruit sapling, and there is a limited amount of resources.

The soil is almost a neutral player in this raging battle between fruit-bearing sprig and voracious vines and weeds.

The soil can support both weeds and fruit. It can aid the good and the bad. You begin to realize you have to think of the garden as a place for a battle strategy. It's all-out war, and you have to prepare yourself for the carnage.

"Fruit tree, soil, weeds," you say, trying to come up with a war plan. You can see that there are two sides, and like every war before, the two sides are fighting over the same patch of ground. The fruit tree wants the soil and its precious resources. The weeds want the soil and its precious resources. They both want the same thing.

"I have to pick a side," you say as you realize the stakes. The battle lines are drawn, so why do you still feel so overwhelmed with the task. You realize you're going to need some advice.

You pull out your phone and go through the contents of your pockets until you find the seed envelope you received from the feed store. You turn it over and look at the handwritten phone number on the back. Aunt Loola had said, "Call me anytime."

You put your phone away and go into the house. It's going to be a battle, but it's a battle for another day.

4
ABUNDANT DEATH

The garden in the story is you. For every believer, you're comprised of at least these three parts. You have a flesh component, a mental component, and a spiritual component.[1] Let's explore the flesh, spirit, and mind each in turn.

FLESH

Thorns, weeds, rocks, and vines represent your flesh and everything that comes with it. Your flesh has desires. Your greatest resources are your time and your talents. If your flesh was allowed to have its way, it would use your *talents* all the *time* to get whatever it desires. Just like the thorns and weeds, the flesh will soak up all of the resources it's allowed to have.

In Jesus' parable of the crop field, he says that the thorny vines are the things that distract people with worries, pleasures, and even riches.[2] Those are the kinds of things the flesh wants—the flesh worries about getting pleasure and getting rich. So, just like the thorns and weeds are in a battle, your flesh is hostile to anything that gets in its way.

Paul tells us what some of the fruits of the flesh are, *Committing sexual sin, being morally bad, doing all kinds of shameful things, worshiping false gods, taking part in witchcraft, hating people, causing trouble, being jealous, angry, or selfish, causing people to argue and divide into separate groups, being filled with envy, getting drunk, having wild parties, and doing other things like this.*[3]

Even weeds bear a kind of fruit. The fruit that the weedy flesh bears is awful. It will wreck you if you let it continue unchecked. This is true of many believers who have let the weeds grow. The thorny plants that will develop in your life bear a terrible kind of seed. Those seeds fall and grow more of the same. It's a vicious cycle that we must fight against. I mentioned three parts. Let's look at your next part.

MIND

The second part of you is your mind, represented by the soil in the story. Just as the soil is the battlefield, so too is your mind.

Before you became a believer, your mind was automatically an ally of your flesh. Just like the soil supports weeds and thorns, the mindset supports flesh-desires exclusively for unbelievers. The unbeliever's mind is close friends with the flesh. All kinds of desires grow in the soil of the mind. Before you were a believer, you would use your mind to find extra clever ways to get what your flesh wanted. You could even do this in ways that made it look like you were doing good. The mind and the flesh are a deadly combination. That's why Paul said, *the mindset of the flesh is death.*[4]

SPIRIT

It wasn't until you became a believer that the third part of you rose from the dead-spiritual ruins. The fruit tree sapling in the story represents the never-ending spiritual life that God placed inside of you the moment you believed. That fruit tree has a powerful purpose. It has an ultimate goal, which we will talk about in the next chapter. In the same way that the fruit tree sapling is at war with the weeds, your spiritual life is in direct competition with your flesh. Why? You might ask.

Because both the fruit tree and the weeds grow in the same soil, your spirit and your flesh are fighting for the same resource, your mind. They are planted in the same dirt. They are warring to gain control of your mind, which is represented by the soil. Just like the soil can either support thorns or fruit-bearing crops, your mind can align with the flesh and allow it to grow, or it can align with the Spirit and allow your inner spiritual life to grow.

The inner spiritual person, which God has brought to life in you, cannot sin.[5] However, your flesh absolutely can sin. Did you catch that? The inner spirit cannot sin, but your flesh does. Maybe you begin to see the problem. Thus, the inner war.

Your sinful flesh and your sinless spirit are at war, and your mind is caught between. The part of you that thinks, is the battleground. As long as the flesh is winning the war, there will be a lack of joy, peace, love, patience, kindness, and the rest. The greedy weeds and thorns suck all of the nutrients out of the soil and block any precious sunlight from getting through. Your flesh wants nothing more than to occupy your mind all the time so that nothing good can grow. If your mind stays aligned with the flesh, you'll have the fruits of the flesh growing in your life. It's an ugly business.

Paul was talking about this when he said, *when I want to do what is right; I inevitably do what is wrong. I love God's law with all my heart. But there is another power within me that is at war with my mind. This power makes me a slave to the sin that is still within me.*[6] Paul said this as a saved believer. If Paul experienced this, so can we.

When your mind is allied with your flesh, it is at war with your spirit and makes your mind enemy territory for God.[7] Can you believe it? All of this is happening inside of you! Hopefully, you're beginning to see why things are the way they are.

Do you experience a lack of peace and joy in your life? Do you experience an abundance of negative emotions? Do you have a lot less patience and kindness than you think you should possess? Are you struggling to gain self-control over certain sins? These are signs that your mind has allied with your flesh and that both are at war with your spirit.

Remember *the mindset of the flesh is death.*[8] Your eternal life can never be taken away now that it's been placed inside of you. Your spiritual never-ending life can never die. However, your chance at an abundant and fulfilling life dies a little more every time your mind is aligned with the flesh. A lack of peace and joy will grow the longer your mind stays focused there.

It's time we learned the ultimate goal of our life. This is an invaluable tool in the fight against the flesh.

5

GARDENING GOAL

You're standing, once again, in that overgrown wood that you can't really call a garden. There is hardly anything redeeming about it. It's packed with rocks and thorns. Vines block out the sun from reaching the ground. The place is a wreck. You've visited the unkempt property for weeks now but haven't seen a change. Once more, you spend the morning staring at the weeds and thorns, trying to get motivated. You have no idea what to do. You reiterate your need for some advice.

You reach for your back pocket, seeing if the seed envelope is still there. You find it and pull it into the sunlight. After flipping it over, your eyes rest on the handwritten phone number scrawled across the envelope flap. The feed store clerk's number is a gardening lifeline. You reach for your phone, and in another second, the line is ringing.

"Hello," a lady says on the other end.

"Garden department, please," you say.

"Well, Honey, you called my kitchen phone. I could go and pick up the one by my bed if you want." The woman says.

“Is this Bart’s Feed Store?” you ask.

“Nope, it’s my house,” she says.

"Oh, sorry, wrong number," you say and hang up embarrassed. You must have typed the digits wrong. You look at the envelope again. Within another few seconds, you've dialed, and the phone is ringing once more.

“Garden department,” a lady’s voice says. You’re almost sure it is the same voice.

“Uh, is this—” you start to say, but she cuts you off.

“Still my house,” she says.

“Oh, I’m really sorry. She must have given me the wrong number or something.”

“Who are you trying to reach?” she asks. You look at the envelope and read the numbers.

“I said, *who* not what number." she says. You glance back at the envelope flap. Before you can read the name, the woman says, "It's written right there next to the number in blue ink."

"Aunt Loola?" you say, letting the question color your tone.

“The one and only.”

“You gave me your personal number?”

“I only work at the feed store one day a week. I always give my home number in case of a gardening emergency.”

“It’s not an emergency,” you say. “It’s just that I— I— have no idea what to do. How do I keep the tree from drying out? How do I make sure I’m not overwatering or under watering? How do I—” you trail off.

“You got to learn to ask the right question first.” she says.

“What do you mean?” you ask.

“See, there you go again asking the wrong question,” she says as she chuckles warmly. You begin to pace in the yard.

"When you first rang my phone, you asked for the garden

department; when you got an answer, you assumed that something had gone wrong. Usually, people are asking the wrong questions." she says.

"Oh, ok," you say, taken aback. This feisty old lady was bold. You smile at her gall.

"Since you're just getting started, I'll give you this one for free," she says. "The question you have to ask is this: what's the goal of your garden?"

"I— uh," you stall out.

"The ultimate purpose of the garden is—" her voice is expectant.

"You kind of caught me off guard there," you say.

"Ok. Is the grand gardening goal to water the right amount?"

"No, I don't guess so."

"That's your first assignment, to figure out what the ultimate goal of your garden is," she says.

"Assignment?" you ask. "I didn't know there would be homework."

"Hey, you planted the seed."

"I know," you say. "I guess I was expecting some advice that is a little more specific."

"You don't need specifics; you need to figure out what your garden's goal is," she says. When you don't respond right away, she adds, "Ok, Honey. Thanks for calling. Call anytime."

The phone beeps, and the call ends. "Well, that was weird," you say, returning your phone to your pocket. You stare at the seed pouch. After a long moment, you glance to the garden, considering what Aunt Loola said.

As bizarre as the conversation was, you see a seed of truth in it. You planted the seed without any consideration for the goal. *What is the goal?* You think. You're pacing now, hand on your chin.

"What is the goal," you say, exasperated. The question swells in your mind. It begs an answer. As you look at the wild patch of overgrowth, the question echos, ringing louder as it morphs and changes. "What's my ultimate goal here?" you say louder this time.

Hidden under the immense tangle of weeds and thorns is the tiniest sprig of a fruit tree. The last time you saw, its growth was stalled by the intense competition. Though it hurts your hands, you part the thorns with your tender palms. Down below the brush, you can see that the sprig is still alive, but it's in danger. If it doesn't find a path to the light, it will inevitably be choked to the point where it can never bear fruit.

"What's my *ultimate goal?"* you say. With a sudden parting of the clouds, you realize the desired result. You see the purpose of the garden, the tree, the battle, the struggle. This single goal will drive you forward. You sharpen your focus and fixate on the one thing that matters. The goal is to bring that fruit tree to fruition. "FRUIT," you shout with joy. "My *ultimate goal* is fruit!" It's like a bit of bottled lightning loosed in your mind. You have a new goal, a new purpose, a new mission.

The grand garden goal is fruit. You want fruit to spring from the tree. You want that sweet outcome. You suddenly feel the goal automatically reorganizing your priorities. You feel invigorated and energized. Realizing the purpose of the garden gives you hope and excitement. The ultimate goal becomes your guiding star. It becomes your compass bearing. It's a great feeling. You reach for your cell and dial.

"It's fruit, abundant fruit!" you nearly shout into the phone. Aunt Loola giggles with excitement as you exclaim.

"That's right. The grand gardening goal is fruit!" she confirms.

"So, now what?" you say, ready to get started.

"Now it's my nap time," she says. You hang up feeling a sense of accomplishment. You've found your purpose.

6
THE GOAL OF YOUR LIFE

Now, are you ready to find out what the ultimate purpose of your Christian life is? Do you want to know God's goal for your life? I've made you wait long enough. Are you ready? Here it is:

ABUNDANT LIFE!

Jesus said that He came to do two things. He came to give life (eternal) and to give life more abundantly.[1] If you've believed in Jesus for eternal life, then the point of you sticking around any longer is to have abundant life. Since you have already received Jesus' gift of eternal life, assuming you're a believer, the next step is to realize that your ultimate goal, the magnificent purpose of your remaining time on this planet, is to have an abundant life.

Paul talked about the same idea when he said, *You belong to him who was raised from the dead in order that we may bear fruit for God.*[2] The goal of your time on Earth as a believer is that you bear fruit abundantly. That's what you're here for.

That's why God didn't just suck you up into Heaven the moment you believed.

Now, some may give a sigh of disappointment, thinking that sounds pretty stuffy and boring. Wait just a moment. This is what you're designed to do. This is what you're here for. Before you leave the garden in a huff, let's see what a fruit-filled abundant life would look like. For that, Paul gives us a simple answer.

Paul said, *the fruit of the Spirit is love, joy, peace, patience, kindness, goodness, faithfulness, gentleness, and self-control.*[3] You should breathe a sigh of *relief.* In fact, you should be jumping up and down right now. The goal of your life is not to be locked into endless prayer meetings or to constantly have your nose in the pages of your Bible. It's not even to check the attendance box at church. The ultimate goal of your life is to have more joy, peace, and love.

Don't you want to have more joy, peace, love, and the rest? Of course, you do. In fact, it's why about fifty billion self-help books are written each year. It's why people are experimenting with eastern meditation. It's why others are chasing the almighty dollar. It's why most people do, well, whatever it is that they do. People want these things.

This is amazing news, right? The goal of your life, according to God's word, is something you already want. Don't we have an impressive engineer that designed us? He made us to want what he designed us to have. He created us to have eternal life, but also to experience that eternal life abundantly.

Imagine for a moment what your life would be like if it were defined by a greater abundance of joy. Really. Stop and think about it for a moment. God's goal for your life is that you be abundantly joyful. What would your life be like if you were fully at peace? Imagine having an abundance of peace in your mind, your relationships, your finances, your job. Life is beautiful when you're at peace. Envision, if you can, that your life was marked by an overabundance of love. How wonderful would that be? The same is true of all of the fruits of the spirit. Life just gets better the more of these fruits that grow in your garden. You won't find these fruits in any other garden. Only in God's Spirit are you going to be able to see this incredible goal develop in you.

Let's answer one obvious question that might come up. Does *Abundant life* mean that we can expect abundant wealth, health, and luxury? Can we anticipate that there will be a complete lack of suffering if we are experiencing abundant life? Nope. You're on Earth, aren't you? You're still going to go through your fair share of troubles and trials. However, you can see the difference that abundant life makes when you go through those trials. Having abundant life means that you'll be able to handle various kinds of suffering while still maintaining joy, peace, and love. You'll be able to maintain self-control and gentleness even when your circumstances are deteriorating. You'll be able to stay faithful in the midst of a world falling apart.

Do you want abundant life? If you have a somewhat fruitful life already, do you want a more abundant life? I know I do. I want my life to be so jam-packed with fruit that I can't hold anymore. I hope that's what you want as well. I hope you're so fruit-hungry that you can already taste it.

We'll get to the *how* in a bit, but first, I want to answer a question that some might ask. In the next chapter, I'll explain why God wants you to have an abundant life.

7
A SELFISH GARDENER

You've spent a few weeks dreaming about fruit, now. Each morning you stand in the place where your fruit tree sapling is planted. You can't wait to see that little sprig spring into a vibrant giant with heavily laden branches of edible delights.

As you sit among the vines and thorns waiting for the fruit tree to grow, you hear someone approaching. You stretch your neck to see above the weeds. Your new neighbor, Gary, is walking toward your garden haven. Though you're new to the neighborhood, you've met Gary once before. You've noticed his morning walks that sometimes stretch into the afternoon, depending on who he stops to talk to.

"What are you doing there?" Gary says. You dust yourself off and reach out your hand to shake. He glances down at your soil-covered palm and offers a fist bump instead. It distracts you from answering, so he rewords his question. "Why are you sitting in that wild patch of weeds? You're not some kind of nature worshiper, are you? We don't go in for that kind of thing around here."

"Oh, no. I'm just waiting to get some fruit from this little fruit tree," you explain, gesturing toward the ground. Gary steps closer and investigates the thorny patch.

"All you're going to get from that is a rash," he says. You glance down.

"Huh?" you ask abruptly.

"That's poison ivy?"

"Oh, no," you say. "Not that. There's a fruit tree that's planted beneath all that stuff."

"Oh, right," Gary says, glancing around with a judgmental look that you don't much like. "Why'd you plant a fruit tree in this mess?" Gary asks. You know the answer to that one. You've spent long hours dreaming about the abundant harvest you'll enjoy.

"My ultimate goal is to have fruit," you explain. Your smile, you assume, communicates your air-tight plan.

"Are you going to share?" Gary asks.

"I— uh—" you stammer. You haven't really thought about it.

"Apples are a buck thirty-two at Gerald's Groceries now. I told them that everyone was going to stop eating apples if they keep raising the price, but they didn't listen." Gary lets out an annoyed grunt. "Anyway, it doesn't seem fair that you'll have free apples while the rest of us have to spend our hard-earned money on overpriced store-bought fruit."

"I don't know how much fruit to expect for the first season," you say. "It might only be a little—"

"Seems kind of selfish," Gary cuts you off. "If you're just going to grow a bunch of fruit and keep it for yourself." You don't have a response.

"Alright, I guess I'll just keep getting my apples the old-fashioned way," Gary says after a long awkward moment of silence. "See ya."

You hardly hear him leave. You're thinking about your goal. You were so excited about coming to an understanding of the garden's purpose, but now you're questioning everything all over again.

Certainly, Gary's manners could use some work, but his questions have unearthed something you haven't thought of. *Why do I want fruit?* Your thoughts wander. *Is it ok for my goal to be enjoying the fruit, or am I just being selfish?* You sit and ponder these questions as the sun rises hot overhead. Before you know it, your phone is in your hand and ringing.

"Isn't it selfish for my ultimate goal to be fruit?" you ask. Aunt Loola laughs.

"Who told you that?" she asks.

"My neighbor came by and accused me of being selfish if I don't share."

"I've got a neighbor just like that," Loola says. "I call him gossiping Gary."

"Wait," you say, surprised. "Gary is the name of the guy I'm talking about."

"What street do you live on?" Loola says.

"Walnut," you say.

"Well, at least I have one good neighbor," she says with a laugh. "I'm on Maple."

"Wow, that's ironic," you say.

"Ok, back to the point," she says abruptly. "Don't worry about Gary. He would have voted for the communists."

"Communists don't do elections, do they?" you say.

"That's kind of my point. He won't work in his own yard, but he'd be happy to take whatever your yard grows."

"Ok, forget Gary. What he said made me think that maybe it is selfish to make abundant fruit my goal."

"Honey, I can tell you when a garden really grows, it makes you generous."

"How's that?" you ask.

"How many serious gardeners do you know?" she asks.

"None," you say but then change your answer. "Well, does knowing you count?"

"You don't know me yet, but yeah. I've known good gardeners all my life. You know what their favorite thing to do is?" she asks.

"What?"

"In the growing season, they are always sharing what their garden grows. When bright, juicy tomatoes, ripe figs, or plump plumbs bud bursting from those sagging limbs, you'll have so much fruit you couldn't eat it in ten lifetimes. The first thing you'll want to do is find more mouths to try what sprouted from your soil. The first thing you'll do is share."

"Probably not with Gary," you say.

"Nah, you'll see. I bet even Gary will get some." she says.

"Don't worry, Honey; gardening is the opposite of selfish."

8

GOD WANTS ABUNDANCE

In the last section, I made the claim that the ultimate goal of your Christian experience is to have abundant life. Abundant life is a life filled with the fruits of the Spirit like love, joy, peace, and the rest. There will be those out there that will complain. They will say, "It seems selfish to make your goal an abundant life."

I'm going to defend your purpose of abundant life by appealing to the highest authority. God wants you to have abundant life as a Christian. It's one of the main reasons that He sent his only son.[1] Though, you might still ask, "why?" Why does God want me to have an abundant life? There are a few reasons.

We can illustrate why with something you've probably noticed. Basically, every ad campaign since the beginning of advertising is based on this concept, from Apple products to camping equipment. Commercials selling these items are packed with happy people having the best time they've ever had. When you see people having a fulfilling and enjoyable time, you will be attracted to the products that make it possible. You'll ask questions like, "how do I get the same fulfillment." The advertiser is ready to supply you with the answer for only $39.99 a month.

Those commercials are only a dim reflection of this basic truth. You are God's greatest advertisement when you are the most fulfilled. When you have an abundant life, you draw people toward the source of your fulfillment, which is God. God wants you to have an abundant life because you become his advertisement campaign to the world.

Imagine the opposite for a second, though. Envision a commercial with people who are angry, bitter, and dissatisfied. How much product do you think that ad campaign will sell? Not much! Frustration, contempt, and discontentment are common feelings. Potential customers don't want to feel these negative emotions, and they will stop at nothing to avoid them. If you, as a Christian, are dissatisfied with your life, it displeases God. It's a wasted opportunity. It's a failed ad campaign. He wants you to be fulfilled so that you can bring others toward Him.

The greatest evangelistic method you can employ is to have an incredibly abundant life. Jesus put it this way, *by this, everyone will know that you are my disciples if you love one another.*[2] Notice that it doesn't say that others will know that you're saved, but that they will know you are a disciple. There's a big difference between salvation and discipleship.[3] Love is one of the fruits of the Spirit. Love for one another is one of the marks that we are experiencing abundant life. That love for one another will signify to outsiders that you are Jesus' disciple. Since the world is so packed with rivalry, bitterness, and hatred, your love will signify that Jesus has a better and more fulfilling way of life for those who follow Him.

I had a friend who used to say, "when you get squeezed, the truth comes out. When you hit trouble in your life, your true character oozes from you." He proved the statement true when he got skin cancer. I talked to him about his terminal diagnosis not long before he died. He said, "Man, if the Lord takes me, then great! It's been a wild ride!" He talked about his impending death with a smile, excitement, and joy.

Something beautiful happened at that moment. I wanted what he had. He was satisfied with his life. He was happy to go home to be with the Lord. It made me want that same kind of abundance. He was a fantastic ad campaign for the Lord.

It'd be easy to think that abundant life is a lack of trouble, but it's quite the opposite. God wants to use your character as a billboard for his life fulfillment program. That means that God may just allow you to experience trouble so that you can demonstrate how satisfied you are in Him. When you find fulfillment in Him, even in the midst of suffering, it will draw other people toward the never-ending source of life and peace.

So when that co-worker hurts your feelings, if you respond with love, patience, kindness, gentleness, and self-control, and they know that you're doing that because you're a Christian, then you are demonstrating a very attractive kind of abundance. That's a successful ad for the Lord. I'm not saying that means a person will suddenly realize they need a relationship with Christ, but it's another sliver of evidence that they do.

Another reason God wants you to have an abundant life is that it glorifies Him. God is glorified by you when you are satisfied by Him. It's one of the greatest proofs that you are in communion with your creator. None of the gods of the ancient pagan religions have ever satisfied those who worshiped them. None of the methods of legalist religion can do it either. Nothing in the world can satisfy except the creator. That's why the Bible says so many times that *the Lord is my portion.*[4] When you're satisfied by God's abundance, it glorifies Him.

In addition, God wants to reward you. It's kind of crazy that not only does He want to reward you here and now for your obedience to Him, but He wants to reward you for it when you arrive in Heaven.[5] That's why the writer of Hebrews says that He is a rewarder of those who diligently seek Him.[6] Those who seek the Lord and find abundant life in Him will also be rewarded for it in the next life.

Is God your portion? Have you found fulfillment in Him? When struggles and trials come, do you ooze Godly character? Are you satisfied, content, and enjoying your Christian life? God wants you to. In the next chapters, I'm going to tell you how to begin accomplishing this abundant life.

9
YOU CAN'T DO IT

By now you've spent weeks staring at the garden. You have checked the fruit tree sapling. It is a tough plant. It continues to survive, but it is far from thriving. In fact, it hasn't grown a single centimeter since shortly after you planted it.

Each time you visit the wild garden, you kneel down to check the progress of your tiny fruit tree. You have been scratched by thorns, tripped by vines, and plagued by the rash of poisonous ivy since you began. Your goal is to see fruit, but you're not sure what to do.

"I need some more advice," you say to yourself. Your first instinct is to reach for your phone, but then you have an idea. You wander somewhat aimlessly out of the garden, through your yard, and down the street. You're looking for another garden, an oasis in the chaos. You scan each house on your block looking for signs of expertise. You spot Gary's place with its characteristic bald yard and flowerless hedges.

You walk the length of Maple Street before you see a house with finely laid flower beds, a manicured lawn, and well-trimmed trees budding with sprouts. You peek over the fence and spot a well-organized garden. Vegetables and fruits of all kinds are growing in orderly rows. This has got to be it. You walk to the house and knock on the door. An elderly lady opens with a smile.

"How can I help you, Honey?"

"Aunt Loola?" you ask, but already you know from her warm, soothing voice.

"Oh, it's you!" she says. She's pushing back the screen door and wraps her arms around you. The hug is grandmotherly and as welcome as any embrace you've had before.

Before you know it, you're sitting in a rocking chair on her porch, drinking iced tea, and talking about gardening.

"I'm just so frustrated," you explain.

"What's got ya down, Honey?" Aunt Loola asks.

"I've been waiting for my fruit tree to grow. No matter how long I sit there, it just stays the same," you say.

"What's your grand gardening goal?" Aunt Loola asks, reminding you of your previous phone conversation.

"Fruit, abundant fruit," you say. "My ultimate goal is to have a big harvest of fruit."

"Good," she acknowledges.

"But I've just got to make it grow?" you say.

"My hearing isn't so great, Sugar. Did you say you plan to force the fruit to grow?" she asks.

"Well, yeah," you admit.

"Sorry. It ain't gonna happen," she says.

"But, my goal is to get fruit. I've got to make that tree grow." Your confidence is waning.

"And how has that worked out so far?" Aunt Loola asks.

You look out over the railing of the porch. *Maybe this was a mistake.* Aunt Loola takes a long sip of tea before continuing. "I have a question for you."

"Ok."

She pauses for another sip. "How does the sapling power its transformation into a fruit-bearing tree?"

"That's easy," you begin. "The sun shines. Photosynthesis takes place. Then—" Loola cuts you off.

"No. How does the *plant* power *its own* change." Loola says.

"Oh, uh—" you say. You take a moment to think about it. "It doesn't power its *own* growth, I guess."

"You guess?" Aunt Loola asks.

"Yeah. The power comes from somewhere else."

"That's right. The plant does not change; it is changed by a power that's not its own. You can't force a plant to transform, but if it's going to bear fruit, it must do exactly that; transform."

"Yeah, I see what you mean," you agree.

"So, how do you make the plant transform," she asks.

"I don't," you respond. Your confidence is growing, but you're still clueless as to what you're supposed to do. "So am I supposed to do nothing at all?"

"You can't do anything at all to make the sapling grow, but you can do things that help the tree connect with its power source," Aunt Loola explains.

"How do I do that?" you ask.

"Come back tomorrow, and we'll talk about it," she explains. You want answers now, but you're happy to be getting somewhere. You thank her for the tea and conversation and head home thinking about your talk with sweet Aunt Loola.

10

TRANSFORMATION

To experience abundant life, you don't need *more effort*; you need transformation. It's not your effort or willpower that makes this transformation, sometimes called growth, happen. It's true that you have a part to play, which we'll discuss in a later chapter, but the power for the transformation you need comes from somewhere else. It doesn't come from your own will, determination, commitment, or physical abilities.

There are many people who have gotten confused and think that the power to change comes from inside the human mind, heart, or psyche. There are even Christians who attempt to change who they are by trying really hard to make it happen. Mantras, repeated rituals, external discipline structures are an attempt at doing this. Someone can, sometimes, experience some behavioral changes, but these flesh-powered attempts don't have what's needed to transform a person.

Paul explained that even he, as a believer, attempted to follow God's law by grit and determination. Notice how he explains a time when he was attempting a flesh-powered transformation. He said, *I would not have known what it is to covet if the law had not said, Do not covet. And sin, seizing an opportunity through the commandment, produced in me coveting of every kind… For I do not understand what I am doing because I do not practice what I want to do, but I do what I hate.*[1]

He explains something we all understand. If I hear a rule like, "don't think lustful thoughts about Suzzy." What am I almost certainly going to do? Well, my flesh is going to hear the name, Suzzy, over the radio of my inner monologue. The flesh then begins to drum up custom-crafted temptations. The more I say, "don't lust," to my flesh, the more I'm tempted to lust. That's the flesh-powered cycle at work. That's what happens when we try to power transformation ourselves. It simply doesn't work.

So you need transformation, but the problem is that *your* attempt to transform *yourself* is always going to fail. That's because, like the fruit tree, you don't have the power to transform yourself. You can't fight the temptation of the flesh with the power of the flesh. Telling yourself not to sin is as good as fighting fire with more fire.

Paul said, *do not be conformed to this world, but be transformed*[2]. The world is full of bad fruit. If you want good fruit, if you want the abundant, fruitful life that God offers, it's going to be His power, not yours, that brings about the transformation. The fulfilled life is only possible if you transform. Where does transformation power come from?

The moment that you believed in Jesus for salvation, whether you knew it or not, God placed his Holy Spirit inside of you.[3] It's God's Spirit that grows the fruit. It's God's Spirit who is living in you, who produces the transformation which leads to abundant life.

You can't make the fruit tree grow, just like you can't force Spiritual fruit to bud and develop through bodily means. The power of the sun brings about the fruit. God's mysterious power is what will bring about transformation in your life.

So if it's God's power that transforms me, I can just sit back and do *nothing,* right? If you want abundant life, you need transformation. Only God's Spirit can power transformation, but you do have a role to play. Your role is to help connect the flesh to the power source. Yeah, you read that right. You need your flesh to be transformed, and God's Spirit has the power to do it.

Transformation doesn't happen automatically, but it is possible for you and me. Note that in talking about transformation, Paul doesn't just say, "be transformed." He says, "be transformed *by...*" and then explains what will allow the transformation to take place. In the next chapters, we'll talk about our role in our own transformation process.

11
SOIL

You wake with the sun streaming through your window and are at your garden in a few minutes. With transformation on your mind, you wonder where to start.

"I thought I might find you here," comes a now familiar voice.

"Hey, Aunt Loola," you say. "What are you doing here?"

"You visited me; I thought I'd return the favor," she says, coming up slowly with her cane in hand. After some pleasant small talk, you get down to business.

"So, what do I need to do now?" you ask. After looking around, Aunt Loola rubs her lower back.

"First thing, I need a chair," she says but then adds, "and I wouldn't argue with some coffee." You rush off to arrange for seating and to make coffee. By the time you return, the sun is climbing through the trees. A gentle breeze pushes the morning fog along. Within a few minutes, you are sitting with your new friend, next to the wild thorn-covered patch of ground, somewhere beneath, a sprig of a fruit tree lives.

"*Now*, what do I need to do?" you ask. Loola simply looks at the mess of vines and tangles of weeds. When she doesn't respond, you start offering up ideas.

"Should I water?" you ask.

"Yes, but not right now. If the water sits only on the surface, the roots won't go deep."

"Should I fertilize?"

"Not yet, you don't want to hurt the sapling's tender feeder roots with fertilizer. That comes later."

"Should I pull the weeds?"

"You'll have to pull some weeds soon, but the weeds are probably entangled with the roots, so let's wait to do that," she says. "The one thing we need to figure out is if the soil is right."

"So, I need to focus on the soil?" you ask.

"Yes," she says. "Soil is like a recipe. It's got to have all the right ingredients."

"So, how do I know if the soil is right?" you ask.

"The soil is where the magic happens. When it's right, the tree will grow. The soil has to be well-drained. Sandy loam is good. Too much clay, rock, or acid, and the tree won't go to fruit."

"So we've got to get the soil right?" you ask again, noticing she hasn't given any actual instructions.

"Yep," she says as she takes a sip of her coffee.

"So, how do we do that?"

"Let's talk about it," she says, placing her coffee cup next to her chair and rising to her feet. "Tomorrow. My place."

12

MINDSET

To have abundant life, you will need to be transformed by God's Spirit. In order to be transformed, there is something relatively simple you must do. Paul explained it when he said, *do not be conformed to this world but be transformed by the renewing of your mind.*[1] The transformation we need comes from a renewed mind. It's your mindset that determines the rate at which the Spirit transforms you.

To gain abundant life through transformation, you must focus your mind on a particular set of ideas. Paul says it this way, *The mindset of the flesh is death, but the mindset of the Spirit is life and peace.* Peace is one of the marks of an abundant life. It's one of the fruits of the Spirit. When you take your mind off of the flesh and its desires and focus on Spiritual things, you will begin to be transformed into an abundant lifer.

Paul explains the importance of the mindset to accomplish life's ultimate goal in another one of his letters to some of his friends in Colossi. In that letter, Paul said, "Set your mind on things above..."[2] Along with this, he gives some examples of things to set one's mind on. He says, "...Seek those things which are above, where Christ is, sitting at the right hand of God."[3]

Some of those *above* things are Christ, where He's at, and the things that are available through Him. *Setting your mind on things above* bears a strong resemblance to the phrase *seek those things which are above.* That's like saying, *set your sights on things above.*

In another letter to a different group of friends, Paul explains what that mindset should look like when he says, "I press toward the goal for the prize of the upward call of God in Christ Jesus. Therefore let us, as many as are mature, have this mind..." Having a Spiritual mindset includes a focus on the reward Christ will give to those who obey.[4] It will often include remembering that Christ could return at any moment.

In that same letter, he offered this as a note on our mindset—Whatever things are true, noble, just, pure, lovely, of good report, any virtue and, anything praiseworthy—think about these things.[5] It's more simple than you might think. Basically, anything that is spiritually valuable is worth thinking about. When you spend your time with a mind focused on spiritually valuable things, you are accomplishing his instructions.

This is what the prophet Isaiah meant when he said, *You keep him in perfect peace whose mind is stayed on you because he trusts in you.*[6] The one who focuses their mind on God, especially considering His trustworthiness, is going to be a peaceful person. Peace is a fruit that only the Spirit can grow.

When you focus on spiritual things, spiritual fruits start to grow. So, if you want to accomplish the ultimate goal of your life, then it's simple. You need to change your mindset, from a mindset of the flesh— which will kill the fruit— to a mindset of the Spirit— which invites the Spirit to produce fruit in you. The result will be an incredibly abundant life.

Simple right? Yeah, it's simple, but it's not necessarily easy. Paul warns over and over of the damage that the wrong mindset will cause. He says that *the mindset of the flesh is death.* Those who suffer spiritual defeat have their *minds set on earthly things.*[7] Those filled with vanity are puffed up because of a *fleshly mind.*[8] He even says there are people who are *always learning but never able to come to knowledge of the truth* who have *corrupt minds.*[9] Every problem stems from the wrong mindset.

Your spiritual success or failure will be determined by your mindset. No one experiences spiritual success with a corrupt mindset, but no one experiences ultimate spiritual failure who has a mind perpetually set on the Spirit. I love how everything can fall squarely under this easy-to-remember rule: *The right mindset transforms, bringing abundant life.*

Though it sounds simple, that doesn't mean it's easy. It's possible to fail at this simple task. Much of the Bible is devoted to bringing believers into alignment with the right mindset. Do you want spiritual success? I know I do. We are going to need to get our minds right. In some ways, this may seem counter-intuitive, so in the next chapters, we're going to talk about why this mysterious method works, and why it's so hard, and what we need to do to improve our spiritual focus.

13

FOCUS ON THE SOIL

You arrive at Aunt Loola's house the next morning with a pen and notepad. You're eager to get instructions. You feel as if you're finally making progress, as you now know where you have to focus.

You knock on the door, but there is no answer. You knock again and wait. You're about to go home disappointed when you hear a whistling sound coming from around the corner. You walk the length of the porch and peek through the back gate. There's Loola, framed in golden sunlight, working among her small orchard of apple trees.

You steal quietly into the garden, careful not to disturb the delicate calm that rests over the place. A cool breeze wanders effortlessly through the trees. The fruit-laden branches dance as if to some unheard song.

"You're here early," Loola says, without looking in your direction.

"I'm here to learn," you say as you admire a healthy apple, almost ready to pick. "It's beautiful here. I wish I had your green thumb."

Holding her hand in the air, she says, "My thumbs are human-colored."

“I just mean—”

“I know, Honey, I’m goofing.” She inspects another branch as she continues. “No, anyone can be a gardener. It’s in our blood.”

“Would you like some coffee,” she asks.

“Sure.”

“Now, I make *real* coffee, not like that weak tan water you fed me yesterday," she says with a grin. She points her cane in your direction, “Do you think you can handle the real thing?”

"Uh, yes, ma’am,” you giggle. "I just made the coffee weak because I didn't want to keep you up for your 11:00 am nap time," you say. Aunt Loola tips her head back and lets out a hardy laugh, one that comes from somewhere deep.

“That’s ridiculous.” She smiles. “My nap isn’t until 11:30.”

You remain in the garden as she goes into the house to get a couple of mugs and returns with them in one hand. In the other, she has a plastic bag. She hands you the darkest brew you've ever seen. "Thanks for the mud," you say. She laughs as she gestures toward the edge of the garden.

You sit on a bench that borders the oasis as you sip the thick coffee. You make small talk for a few minutes before you turn the conversation toward what you’ve come for.

“You told me I need to focus on my soil,” you say. “What do I need to do?”

"Come with me," she says as she rises to her feet. She carries a bag as she maneuvers through the gardened path. On the other side of the garden, she comes to a large barrel big enough to crawl inside, though you wouldn't want to. Glancing down into the barrel, you see rich dark compost.

"Coffee grounds," she says as she holds the baggie up to

open. She dumps the clump of wet, spent ground coffee beans into the compost barrel.

“Why are you putting those in there?" you ask when her explanation is long in coming.

"They add organic material to the compost and aerate the soil," she explains. You pull out your pen and pad, planning to write, but she places her hand over the page. "But, grounds are also acidic, so if you have acid-loving plants, it's fine, but if you are trying to grow a fruit tree, most don't like too much acid."

"Ok, so less acid," you say, about to jot down the tip.

“No,” she says abruptly. “I'm not trying to give you specifics. I'm trying to teach you a general rule.”

“Oh, sorry. What's the rule?”

"Your fruit tree is in a fight against everything else that wants to use the soil,” she says as she uses the end of her cane to mix the coffee grounds into the rich compost.

“So, I need to make sure the tree has what it needs in the soil?” you ask.

"Yes, but there's more to it than that. Right now, your soil is neutral. It's trying to support both the weeds and the fruit tree. You need to make the soil an alley of the tree and an enemy of the weeds."

“Ok,” you say, begging more.

"There are a handful of things you can do to help align the soil with the tree while choking out the weeds."

“Like what?” you ask.

“We'll get to specifics in a bit. I want to make sure you understand the concept.”

“I understand.”

“Ok, pop quiz,” she says. “How do you make the tree grow?”

“I don't,” you say.

“Good. What empowers the plant to grow?”

“The tree’s growth is powered by the sun,” you say.

“So?”

“So, there’s nothing I can do to force it to grow.”

“Then what are you supposed to do in the garden?” she asks.

“I’m supposed to make the soil an alley of the tree and an enemy of the weeds.”

“Well done,” she says as she folds up the coffee ground bag and tucks it into her gardening apron. She turns and knocks her cane against the barrel to clean it.

“So, what specific things can I do to alley the soil with the tree?”

“First,” she smiles. “Make your coffee stronger.”

You pull out your pen to take down a note. “So that I can use the grounds in the soil?”

"No, because I'm working at the feed store tomorrow, and I'll want a hot cup mid-morning, maybe about 10:30,” she says.

“You want me to meet you at the feed store?”

"Yes, bring coffee and money. I'm going to sell you some things," she says. "I'm a slick salesman." She winks as she stands and heads home.

14

WHY IT WORKS

Your mindset is vital because it blocks you from thinking certain things. This is where the gardening analogy comes in handy. The soil represents the mind. The soil can only support a limited amount of growth. That growth can be weeds, or it can be fruit-bearing plants. Since weeds grow much easier than fruit trees, an attempt to grow both fruit and weeds will result in no fruit but plenty of weeds. If you try to grow both, the crop will fail.

The mind is similar. Because of the limitations of the mind, you can't think of multiple things at once. There is only room in your stream of consciousness to be focused on one thing. What you're focused on can change rapidly, but at any given moment, you are only thinking of one thing at a time. That's a good thing because it allows for some pretty amazing results when you drive your train of thought in a deliberate direction.

Let's think about what Paul said to his friends in Philippi. He said, whatever things are true, noble, just, pure, lovely, of good report, any virtue, and, anything praiseworthy—think about these things.[1] How much time could you fill up thinking about the things Paul mentions here? You could let your mind focus on what's true, noble, pure, lovely, good, and virtuous all day long every day and not run out of thought material.

We must pack our minds so tight with good things that no garbage can fit. I remember my mom used to say, "go occupy yourselves with something productive," to my brothers and me when we were too destructive in the house. Idleness often got us into trouble. She knew if we were occupied with something productive, it would keep us from getting into trouble.

Your mind works in a similar way. If it is not occupied, it can drift back to that old default, which is to focus on fleshly desires. If your mind is so filled with spiritually valuable ideas that nothing else can fit, then you're on your way to spiritual transformation.

If you stock the pantry with good wholesome food so much so that there is no room for chips, cookies, and candy, then when you get hungry, you'll eat what's good. You need to have enough stored away in the pantry of your mind that you can have a focus feast at any time. When the mind is full of good things, it has no room for junk.

No doubt, you've heard the idiom, "an idle mind is the devil's workshop." That illustrates what we're talking about pretty well. If you leave open space in your mind, the flesh can use that space for its own purposes. What's worse, if you fill your mind with fleshly content, the flesh will be that much quicker to occupy your mind. However, if you pack every room with good, not letting your mind be idle for a moment, then your flesh doesn't have as much chance to draw your mind away.

Paul explains it this way, *those who live according to the flesh set their minds on the things of the flesh, but those who live according to the Spirit, the things of the Spirit.*[2] There is a cycle at play here. If your goal is to satisfy your bodily desires, then your mind can stay right where it is, focused on the flesh. When you're mind is focused on the flesh, it will feed the cycle, and it will shove you into a repeating loop. Focus on the flesh will lead to living by the flesh, which will lead to focusing on the flesh, which will lead to living by the flesh.

However, when your mind moves to the spiritual realm when you focus on Godly things, it unlocks this amazing new level. A new cycle begins to take root. When your mind begins to change, it starts to transform you. You begin taking actions that are spiritually motivated, which leads to more focus on the Spiritual subjects. The cycle strengthens the more you do it.

Something amazing happens when you focus your mind on Godly things. You begin to be transformed, which results in abundant life. Fruit begins to grow from your proverbial branches. Things change when you focus on God. When your mind is set on spiritual things God releases his transformation power into you.

Paul explains, *Since the Spirit of Him who raised Jesus from the dead dwells in you, He who raised Christ from the dead will also give life to your mortal bodies through His Spirit who dwells in you.*[3] This is why *the mindset of the Spirit is life and peace.* God, who has experience with raising people from the dead, will use that same kind of resurrection-power in you when you focus your mind on Him. It's a resurrection miracle.

Inside you, there's a power plant humming with limitless renewable energy. It so pleases God when you focus on Him that he allows that power to radiate out even into your flesh. He begins to bring your flesh to life. The transformation begins to permeate your body which was previously dead in the sense that it couldn't do good works. That means that even your flesh will begin to do things that are aligned with the Spirit. It's all because you have a resurrection power plant in your inner being. Your mindset is how you plug in and throw the big switch.

You provide the mindset, and the Spirit provides the transformation power. Your mindset alone would have no power against the flesh if God's Spirit wasn't at work each time you think of Him. When you go to God in your thoughts, He comes to you with transformation power. The Spirit is where fruit and abundant life come from.

Every Christmas, my kids get a number of battery-powered toys. Eventually, those batteries run down. Instead of having an easy-to-open battery compartment, the safety-crazed toy makers manufacture the toys such that you have to have a tiny screwdriver and about seven hours of free time if you want to change the batteries. So, those toys remain dead, not able to do what they were originally designed to do.

As believers, when our minds are set on earthly and fleshly things, we are like those dead-battery toys. We can't do anything worth a good. However, setting our minds on spiritual things is the equivalent of plugging your dead-battery body into a new power source. It's a Frankenstein wiring job. God's Spirit brings life to your dead-battery flesh, making it able to do good, and please God. This is why God gets credit for any good deed you've ever done. It's His Spirit that makes you capable in all cases.

This is why I can say you don't make fruit grow, but you do provide the soil for it to grow from. Your spiritual mindset is the good soil, God's Spirit-power is the sunshine. Those who remain resistant to God will keep their minds on bodily desires and continue to miss out on the transformation He offers. Those who focus their minds on Him are in store for fruit.

Now you might be thinking, "It couldn't be that simple. I'm just supposed to think about God and related subjects, and I'm going to begin to transform into a more spiritual person?" Absolutely. That's why it's such a miracle! However, you ought not miss this important point. I've said it already, and I'll say it again. It's simple, but that doesn't mean it's easy.

The amount of abundant life you will experience is all about how long you can sustain focused on Spiritual things. Every believer can focus on the Godly concepts for at least a little while. Even a person that has only been a Christian for a few seconds can focus on spiritual ideas for a time. However, the success will only come in short bursts, without some training.

What's the longest you have ever been able to keep your mind focused on God? Maybe a few minutes. Possibly an hour here or there. Ultimately our flesh is so good at distracting the mind from God that we don't spend that much time focused on Him. We need practice. We need stamina training.

15

CONDITIONS ARE RIGHT

You arrive at the feed store at ten thirty with a thermos of coffee in hand. You head straight for the gardening section in search of Aunt Loola. She's finishing up with a customer when you arrive. The customer leaves with a cartload of gardening supplies.

"Can I help you?" she says with a wink.

"You are a slick salesman," you say as she pats you on the shoulder. "Here's your jug of the addictive substance, as requested." You hand her the thermos filled with the dark caffeinated drink.

"You're so sweet," she says.

"But what's in there is bitter," you say.

She takes a long draft before nodding. "Just like I like it." She screws the cap on. "Right, let's get to it." You follow her as she begins to walk at the top speed her cane will allow. She quizzes you as you walk.

"What's the goal of the garden?"

"Fruit, abundant fruit!" you say with complete confidence.

"And what power do you have to force a tree to grow?"

“None,” you respond.

“So, what do you do?”

“Focus on the soil,” you say.

“And what do you know about good soil?" she asks.

“It’s black,” you say. She stops in the aisle.

“Nothing,” she says wryly. “‘I Know nothing about good soil,’ is what you meant to say. This will all go much quicker if you don’t pretend to know what you’re talking about.”

"Wow, you are a fantastic salesman. I bet you sell a lot of rakes with that tone," you say, trying to match her sarcasm. She giggles as she turns and begins to walk again.

"Soil plays the most important role. More than anything else, it's what determines how the plant will grow. It purifies, stores, and provides water for the plants. If your soil isn't right, then the plant won't grow."

"So, how do I get it right?" you ask.

"Not by interrupting me," she says.

“Soil has three main parts. Sand, silt, and clay.” She grabs a black water hose from the shelf and puts it into your hands.

“I already have a garden hose,” you say.

“With holes in it?”

"No, of course not."

“That’s why you need this one. It’s got holes in it,” she explains.

“I don’t—”

"Depending on the proportion of sand, silt, and clay, you will have to condition the soil,” she says. "For the first growing season, you have to water consistently." She points her finger in the middle of your chest. "You water the soil, not the plant." She moves her finger down to the hole-filled hose. "This is a drip irrigation hose. It waters the—"

“Soil,” you say.

"That's right. You can't make the plant grow; you can only

make the soil conditions right," she pauses next to a row of similar-looking bags. She scans them quickly before pulling one from the shelf. It has the large red words, *fruit fertilizer* printed across its front. She lays the large bag across your open arms before walking again.

"So, I gather that I will need to fertilize," you say.

"When needed," she says. "Put too much fertilizer on some plants, and they will leaf up but won't bear a single thing to eat. On most it just burns the foliage and ruins the crop."

"How do I know how much to fertilize?" you ask.

"We'll get to that later." She walks on. Around the corner, she holds up a gardening gardening hoe and shovel. "Do you have items that look anything like these?" she says.

"What are those? I've never seen their likeness," you say in mock surprise. "I'm not a complete idiot, you know."

"That wasn't the question," she says.

"No, I don't have a hoe," you admit with shame. She lifts the shovel higher in question. "No, I don't have one of those mysterious items either." She lays them across your overburdened arms.

"So, to get the soil conditions right, you have to water, fertilize, and—"

"Wait?" you guess.

"No," she says. "Weed. You're going to get very good at weeding. That's what the gloves and shovel are for." You follow her to the checkout counter.

As she rings up the total, you say, "I'm not quite sure how to—"

"It's alright, Honey. I'm off for the next few days. I'll come by and walk you through it," she says.

"Thanks for the help," you say as you gather your things and begin to move toward the door.

"Hey, what would you think of taking a ride with me tomorrow morning?" she asks.

"Where to?" you ask.

"Come get me a 4:30."

"Did you say morning?" you vacillate. "I'm not usually up by—"

"It'll be worth it, Honey. There are some things I want to show you before we go all-in on your garden."

16

THE CONDITIONS

To keep the fruit tree growing, you need to work the soil. Good soil needs water, weeding, and fertilizer. In a similar way, there are some activities that will help you keep your mental soil in good condition for spiritual growth. The sun powers the plant while the soil supports it. In the same way, the Spirit powers transformation, leading to abundant life, as your mindset supports the process. It's the Spirit's job to grow the fruit; it's your job to tend to the soil, which is your mindset.

To do that, God offers a few helpful habits. Pretty much everything that will help you stay focused fits into these three categories: 1. Prayer, 2. Scripture, and 3. Fellowship.

For the maximum crop of fruit, you have to water, weed, and fertilize. For the best mindset conditions, you need to pray, fellowship with believers, and learn from God's word. Performing these helpful habits isn't the ultimate goal; they are the methods that foster healthy spirit-oriented thinking. A spiritual thought-life releases His power into your life, which will bring abundant life.

PRAYER

You need to get good at keeping your mind focused on higher things. The first tool for doing this is prayer. In a later section, we will take a look at how Jesus taught us to pray.

SCRIPTURE

If you only ever prayed, it would be like weeding the garden but never watering it. Scripture is a powerful tool to strengthen your mindset. We'll explore why this matters and how to use it in a forthcoming section.

FELLOWSHIP

There is one last category of helpful habits that will strengthen your ability to keep your mind in the right place. You need fellowship with believers. In an upcoming section, we'll take a look at what comes with fellowship and what ways you can succeed in this area of your life.

We will explore the helpful habits of prayer, fellowship, and scripture in a bit, but first, I'd like to take you through some common gardening mistakes.

PART II
GARDENING MISTAKES

17

TOO MUCH SOWING SEEDS

Your car pulls up in front of Aunt Loola's house far earlier than you prefer to be awake. Though you have an urge to lean grumblingly against the horn, she emerges from the font door before you have the car in park.

"Where to?" you say when she gets in the passenger side. She points forward as she buckles up and rests a leather bag on her lap. You pull forward as she unclasps the latch on the satchel. From it she pulls the biggest pair of binoculars you've ever seen. "Is espionage on the agenda?"

"Turn left," she says ignoring your quip. She guides you through the city streets still lit by lamp light. You're on the edge of town now. "Park right down there."

"In that cul-de-sac?" you ask. She already has the binoculars to her face. You put the car into park and look at her, waiting for an explanation. Columns of orange light drive skyward as she twists the reticle.

"Here," she says finally handing the binoculars to you. They are heavier than they look.

"Who am I spying on?" you ask.

"A doubtful gardener," Aunt Loola says. She points down the hill which the cul-de-sac is perched atop. On the other side of the sloping field there are houses that back up to a row of abandoned lots. You twist the ring and bring the view into sharp focus. In the back yard of one of the houses a man is standing staring at the ground. As the morning light emerges on the horizon you can see that the yard around him is covered in knee high grass, weeds, and vines of all kind. It's a mess ever as bad as the so-called garden you keep.

"Another beginner?" you ask. Loola doesn't immediately respond, but begins looking through her bag. "And I thought I was your only student." From her bag she produces a small photograph and hands it to you.

"He was much younger then," she says. In the photo a young man in his mid twenties stands next to a much more youthful Aunt Loola. The photo reveals a freshly tilled base of soil. The two of them wear gardening gloves and smile widely under a lively sunlit sky. The photo is faded from age.

You hand the photo back and retrain the binoculars once again. The man is still staring at the overgrown ground of his backyard. While you watch he reaches a hand in his pocket and pulls out a little paper envelope. You recognize its type. He dumps a handful of seeds into his hands, and scatters them on the weedy ground before him. You furrow your brow and glance back to the photo in Aunt Loola's hand.

"That's the same guy?" you ask.

"Yep,"

"Why does his garden look so awful? And why is he just now planting seeds?"

"He's been doing the same thing for about fifteen years now."

"Doing what?"

"Doubting."

"Doubting what?"

"He doubts what he can't see," Loola said.

"I don't understand," you say as you hand the binoculars back to Loola. She holds them up to her eyes and takes a long look. She then rests them on her lap and takes a deep breath.

"When I first met him, he was excited. He wanted to plant a garden that would add some color to his family's dinner table. I watched him plant the first seeds with my own eyes. He had this beautiful row of fruit tree saplings."

"As time went on he let the garden go a little wild. It was a bit of dollar weed, some crabgrass, nothing we couldn't handle if he would have called me. More time passed and he kept ignoring the weeds. Eventually the saplings we'd planted were completely covered up. He couldn't see them any more."

"Why didn't he just pull the weeds?" you ask.

"That would make too much sense. He should have called me, but instead he had his cousin come over to look at the overgrown plot."

"Is his cousin a gardener?"

"No," she says as if it were an insult to imply such. "He's a lawn boy. He severs all plants at an indiscriminate 1.5 inches with a gas-powered grass murdering machine."

"What do you have against lawn mowers?" you ask.

"Don't change the subject," she says. "So his lawn cutting cousin came calling and sliced down his gardening future."

"The cousin mowed the garden?"

"No. Pay attention."

"Ok, sorry. What did his cousin do?"

"His cousin walked out and said, 'what garden? I don't see no garden!' All I see is a yard needs mowin'."

"Ok," you respond, not quite seeing the relevance.

"He tried to argue but his cousin hit him with this little

gem. 'If fruit you don't spot, a garden, it is not.' He tried to explain he had planted fruit trees but his cousin had a whole slew of expert sayings. 'If fruit don't grow, it's just a yard to mow.' and 'If fruit ain't seen, then it's just a weed.'"

"That one doesn't even rhyme," you say trying to rise to Loola's tone.

"Well, rhyme or not, it sowed the seed of doubt," Loola said.

"Why didn't you straighten him out?" you ask.

"I tried. About a week after his cutting cousin did his damage I came around for some sweet tea. I asked him how his fruit garden grows. He informed me that he didn't have a garden, but he was hoping to start one soon. I was as confused as a baboon in a spelling bee. I told him he had a garden, I was there when it was planted, but he didn't budge. I got down on my hands and knees, parted the weeds, and pointed out the row of saplings."

"Certainly that changed his mind," you say.

"Not a wink. You know what he said to me?"

"What?"

"If you can't see fruit, it's a weed's shoot."

"Well at least that one rhymes," you say.

"What is the world coming to. Just because something sounds like poetry doesn't mean it's true. I guess no one ever told him that nonsense can rhyme too. But he believed the rhyme. He won't believe he's got a fruit tree until he sees actual fruit. It's ridiculous."

"So, is that why he's throwing more seed on the ground?" you ask.

"That's what he does every morning around sunrise. Since he doesn't see any fruit he just keeps trying to sow seed. Over and over. He's probably dropped a thousand pounds of seed on that ground."

"I bet he's popular with the birds," you say.

"As long as he doesn't see fruit, he'll just keep trying to start a new garden. It's because he doubts the existence of what he already has that he can't get what he has to grow."

"I feel like I'm supposed to learn something from this," you say.

"Don't expect it to rhyme."

"Ok."

"The point is simple: Believe the label."

"The label?"

"When you get started you ought to put garden markers in. A marker is a little label that says what you planted in each spot. If the label says there's a fruit tree there, then there's a fruit tree there even if you can't see its fruit. It's true that once the tree bears fruit, you can identify it by what it bears. Until is buds, though, you have to know what's planted or you won't be able to give it what it needs. Or worse, if you don't know for sure you've got a fruit tree sapling, then you might wind up trying to reseed it over and over."

"So, you're saying I need to have assurance."

"That's right! You need to have certainty that the tree is there and wants to grow fruit. Without that, you'll just keep running circles around the same patch of overgrown land trying to seed ground that is already seeded.

"Now for something even more important," Loola says. "I'd like some breakfast."

"Seems like a fair trade for such *sage* advice," you say as you put the car into drive.

"You'd have to have a herb garden for me to give you *sage* advice," she says giggling with pleasure at her own wit.

18
NO FRUIT NO ROOT

I can't count the number of times I've heard preachers and Bible teachers pressure a congregation to doubt their salvation. I've heard pastors use phrases like, "If there's no fruit, there's no root." What they mean by this is simple. If you're not doing good works, you must not be saved. Any botanist could tell you, however, that a lack of apples doesn't mean an apple tree is missing its roots. The analogy is not good theology and is likely repeated for only one reason: because it rhymes.

Jesus himself used the analogy of a fruit-bearing plant to represent the life of a Christian. Do you think it's possible that Jesus was aware that sometimes fruit-bearing plants don't bear fruit? Of course, he was aware of that! He is the author of life! In fact, he encountered a figless fruit tree in Judea.

It's interesting Jesus used such an analogy. There are some crops that produce the very same year they're planted, but fruit trees can take years to grow and have entire seasons where no fruit is produced. That means that not only is it possible for there to be times in Christian's lives where there is no Spiritual fruit, it's almost a given. It's built into the analogy. You can't look at a lack of fruit (good works) to prove that a person is not saved. Likewise, you can't prove that a person was never saved in the first place by a lack of fruit.

There are so many Bible-thumping preachers who would have you doubt your salvation on a daily basis. I've actually heard preachers say that doubting your salvation is healthy. On the contrary, it's quite the opposite.

If you've believed in Jesus for salvation, then you have it. You can't lose it. It's yours forever. I've spent a substantial portion of my life writing books about this subject. If you'd like to explore the free gift of everlasting life that Jesus promises you, I'd invite you to read one of them.[1]

Assuming you've believed in Jesus for the free gift of everlasting life, then you never need to doubt your salvation again. To doubt your salvation after believing in Jesus' promise of eternal life is to doubt that Jesus is telling the truth. Now I'll ask you, what Spiritual good can come from doubting Jesus? None at all!

The real danger of salvation-doubt is that it is a self-enforcing cycle. When someone doubts that Jesus has saved them, that person inevitably begins to look elsewhere for proof of their salvation. The only place they can look is to their own works (fruit) to try to find reassurance that they are saved. What often happens is the person doesn't find the kind of fruit they are looking for, and then they doubt even more. Doubt is the opposite of a mind set on spiritual things.

The problem is not that you lack salvation but that you lack fruit. Recall the doubtful gardener from the story. He had misdiagnosed the garden's problem and kept trying to seed the garden when what he really needed to do was begin to work on the garden's condition to make it fruit-ready.

Salvation-doubt becomes a cycle because you keep questioning whether you're saved rather than questioning why you're not bearing fruit. It keeps your attention from being focused on the very thing you need to focus on in order to bear fruit. This is why I'm convinced that one of the most powerful tools the devil can use to keep Christians from experiencing abundant life is to have them regularly listen to a preacher that makes them doubt their salvation.

Doubt of salvation results in a non-abundant life. Since the grand goal of your remaining time on earth is to experience abundant life, it's time you put your salvation-doubts to rest. It's time you become convinced that Jesus' promise of free eternal life for all those who believe in him for it is true and trustworthy.

In case you're a little hazy about what Jesus promised you, take a look at these words from John's gospel. *He who believes in Me [Jesus] has everlasting life*[2] *...I give them eternal life, and they will never die. And no person can steal them out of my hand.*[3]

Jesus' promise is absolute. If you believe in Him for that free gift which He is offering, then you have it as soon as you believe. Everlasting life can't be earned, returned, or lost. Once you believe in Jesus for salvation, you never need to doubt again.

If you keep doubting, you will struggle to bear spiritual fruit. Jesus offers abundant life only after you have eternal life. To take hold of that abundant life, you need to regain assurance in His promise of eternal life.

19

FORGETTING THE PURPOSE

You show Aunt Loola around the house and offer her a seat at the kitchen table. You start a dark pot of coffee brewing and pull out some eggs and a skillet.

"So, are we going to work in the garden today?" you ask as she shuffles into the kitchen.

"I am concerned," she says.

"About?"

"Have you ever heard the story of the gardener who forgot his purpose?" Loola asked.

"Nope," you say as you pull the pan from the stove. "But I have a feeling I'm about to." Loola begins to talk as you prepare the breakfast.

"There once was a gardener who didn't know what he was doing."

"Sounds familiar," you mumble.

"His ground was overgrown with weeds and rocks strewn all around. Thorns choked anything that attempted to climb toward the sky. The spread of wild vines and thistles was daunting. Each morning he would stare out the back window at his garden and feel intimidated by the sight of it. 'How am I going to handle such a mess,' he would ask himself."

"Sounds *very* familiar," you say as you set a plate before Loola and pour the coffee.

"He knew he needed to be disciplined, hard-working, and diligent. So he began to make a plan. The problem was, he didn't know the ultimate goal." Loola pauses and catches your eye. "What's your ultimate goal in the garden?" she asks squarely.

"Fruit. Abundant fruit!" You sing it out with confidence.

"That's right," Loola says, but this so-called gardener didn't know the ultimate goal of gardening."

"Uh, oh. I sense trouble," you say as you take a chair across from Loola and grab your fork. You both pause to say grace before she proceeds with the story.

"So this clueless want-to-be gardener didn't know the goal of a garden, so he improvised. He had seen other gardeners water their garden. 'I'll spend fifteen minutes a day watering,' he said to himself. He was proud to have a plan, a purpose, a goal."

"Sounds reasonable," you say.

"Sounds can be deceiving," Loola says as she stuffs eggs into her mouth. The story is apparently too important for her to wait to swallow.

"On the first day, he waters twenty minutes in his garden. The second day he does thirty. The third he does an hour. It's easy, and the weeds and thorns love the cool drink. He feels a sense of accomplishment, but he's already made a fatal mistake."

"Fatal?" you say. "Did he eat the red berries?" Loola ignores your interjection.

"He feels so productive that he makes watering an hour

per day his new garden goal, his priority purpose, his major mission." She points her fork in your face from across the table. "What is the goal of the garden?"

"Fruit!" you cry with mock passion.

"Not this guy. His sole purpose was to water. He'd completely lost sight of the fruit at the finish line."

"So what happened then?" you say.

"After a week, he began to see a problem. The weeds had grown like crazy. The thorns were sharper. He was frustrated. Angry. Tired. So, he decided that he needed to adjust his garden goal. He shifted his garden goal into overdrive. He committed to water two hours every day."

"Water bill was probably getting a bit outrageous,"

"One day, he got a call from some friends who wanted to go bowling. He loved bowling, but he declined the offer."

"Why?"

"Because his mission is to spend three hours a day watering," she says as she takes another bite.

"I thought you said it was two hours a day," you reply.

"It was, but he had to up it again because the garden was going wild."

"So he didn't want to go bowling?" you say, to get the story back on track.

"No, he wanted to go bowling, but he snubbed the invite because he had to spend four hours a day watering the garden."

"Four hours," you start, but then let it go.

"As he poured gallon after gallon into the weedy pit of mud, he tried to convince himself that ignoring his friends was the right thing to do. He grumbled as he rained down the splashing flow, 'Gardeners have more important duties than bowling. Gardeners have to water. That's a gardener's goal, to be so busy watering that they can't do anything else. If a gardener spends any time doing anything but watering, he should feel really guilty.' After a while, he started to despise his friends for going bowling. He thought they should be in their gardens watering five hours a day as well."

"This guy was really missing the point," you say.

"After a few months, goat weed and poison ivy had taken over his beloved garden. The ground, if you could see it through the weeds, was a swamp. After a while, his friends stopped inviting him to join them for social outings. He'd been watering incessantly, but his so called-garden looked worse than it ever did."

"Yikes."

"Yeah, he was in a real pickle. One day he came to his senses, sort of. He thought to himself, *Well, I've tried gardening, and it just doesn't work for me.* His garden was such an incredible embarrassment; he could only see two options ahead. He could quit *gardening*, or he could continue doing what he's doing and *pretend* it was working."

"What did he decide?" you ask.

"That's not how this story works," she says. "We're to the moral of the story, so there's no more story. Now I repeat the point, and you nod while saying 'oh wow,' or something like that."

"Oh right," you say, clearing your throat.

"Yes and," she sits waiting.

"Oh, wow," you say, intentionally overacting your part. "I see what you're trying to teach me."

"Overdoing it a little, but I'll take it. So, what went wrong?" she asks.

"He forgot the goal," you say.

"And what is this grand gardening goal?"

"Fruit, glorious fruit!" you exclaim as you knock your fork against your now empty plate.

“That’s right. He took what should have been a helpful habit and turned it into the ultimate gardening goal. As soon as he lost sight of the prize at the end of the season, his goal became fluid.” She smiles, clearly proud of her pun. You can’t help but mirror her grin.

“I see what you did there,” you say.

"The goal has to be a fixed, unchanging point, or you'll flounder. Fruit has to be the ultimate goal, or you'll lose your way. So, that's the story of the gardener who forgot the goal."

“Well, are we ready to get out there and work for some fruit?" you ask.

“No, we have to do something more important first.”

“What,” you say.

“The dishes,” she stands and moves toward the sink.

20
DON'T FORGET

Do you realize that this is where many Christians are? They've taken what were supposed to be *helpful habits* like praying, study, and attendance, and they've turned them into the ultimate goal. They've converted the Christian life into a to-do list. Though they are checking off tasks from their list, they are not growing. The main reason for this is because they have forgotten their ultimate purpose. They don't know the goal of the Christian life. Are you living out a defeated Christian life? Have you ever come to realize that you are doing a lot of Christian tasks but seeing very little reward for your effort? Many Christians are on the one, one, one plan. They pray one minute, read one chapter a day, and do one hour in church a week. They think of this as the ultimate goal of the Christian life. They assume these tasks represent the main purpose of being Christian.

Each of these tasks have their place, but they are not the goal. If you turn these tasks into the ultimate goal, your Christian life is going to be incredibly tiring, boring, and insipid. In fact, if you turn the manual habits into the ultimate goal, you're in danger of quitting or pretending it is working. Be careful to keep your goal in mind. So what would forgetting the goal look like?

If you forget your ultimate goal, there are basically two paths you will take. The first one is the *lazy loaf* path. If you forget your ultimate goal, it will become easy to cheat on the tasks. You'll get to where you only pray at mealtimes because the kids are watching. You'll pretty much just look at your Bible when you're at church. You'll get to where you only go to church on the holidays.

Confusing tasks for the goal means that you will deplete your energy. You will feel fatigued. You'll tire of praying, reading your Bible, attending church, and all the trappings that come with them? Whether you openly admit it or not, you will become bored with the Christian life.

Eventually, you'll start thinking of quitting altogether. You'll get bitter about all of the expectations that fellow Christians are placing on you, and you'll start to look for reasons to become very scarce at any faith-based functions. If you see yourself in any of the above words, then you're on a well-worn path, and it's time to make a change.

If this is you, then you've noticed another thing as you've gotten more tired, haven't you? You used to work hard to keep sin out of your life, but now those same old sins are creeping in. You don't want to tell anyone, but they are growing, and you don't know what to do about it. You tell yourself to stop! You try to focus on quitting that bad habit, but that just makes you focus on the sin more, which leads to doing it more.

Paul talked about this when he said, *I found that the very commandment that was intended to bring life actually brought death.*[1] After he became a believer, he noticed that the more he tried to motivate his body to *follow the rules*, the less spiritual success he experienced. He became trapped by the habits and got stuck in this cycle. He'd tell himself not to lust after so-and-so, but that would make him think about so-and-so, so he'd lust for her more. He got so frustrated by being trapped by the habit that he finally said, *O wretched man that I am! Who will deliver me from this body of death?*[2]

Being *trapped by habits* is draining. When you forget your goal, it's easy to get trapped into an endless cycle of empty habits, both good and bad. In that case, the Christian life becomes an endless parade of seemingly meaningless tasks which never satisfy any purpose other than to get your Christian friends off your back. As you grow more weary, bad habits grow. Sin increases.

There's another possible path that you might have taken. If you didn't become the *lazy loaf*, then you might have followed another equally dangerous route. Many Christians have forgotten or never knew the ultimate goal of their Christian life. As a result, they improvised by taking all of those helpful habits like prayer, study, and attendance and converted them into absolute laws. This person I call the *lifestyle legalistic.* They may say that God's grace is free, but they act like you have to earn it. They look down on anyone that can't live up to their standard, and they are secretly bitter at anyone they have to look up to. This mentality is a breeding ground for pride and jealousy. It leaves them with a lack of real fruit and hurts those around them.

If all of this is true of you, you're another victim of legalism. I know, I know. You don't think of yourself as a legalistic, but it's way more common than you think. My personal definition of legalism is when you take what is supposed to be a *helpful habit* and turn it into an *ultimate purpose.* It's taking the means and making it the end. That, in a very loose sense, is legalism. Legalism in the Christian life will rob you of your energy and excitement. I want to set you free from it.

Are you trapped by habits as you watch your emotional batteries slowly drain, or you dive deeper into what feels like legalism? Whichever is true of you; you need freedom! You need to stop thinking of prayer, study, and attendance as the ultimate goal. That as a goal will lead you to some strange and unfriendly places. We'll talk about those things later, but for now, just put them on the shelf.

The ultimate goal of the garden is fruit, fruit, and more fruit. We'll talk about how to do that in a bit, but first, let's tackle another common gardening problem.

21
GOAL SWAP

You dry As Aunt Loola washes the dishes. After a moment, you notice a smile stretch across her face.

"Hey, do you have time to go see a friend of mine?" Loola asks.

"Sure, why not," you say. You grab your keys and escort Aunt Loola to the car. She directs you toward the interstate, explaining that her friend lives in the next town over. You chat as you drive.

"You know when I got started gardening, I wasn't so different from you?" she says.

"Oh really?"

"Yeah, I actually did what you did," she said. "I planted my first fruit tree right in the middle of an overgrown patch of weeds. I had no idea what I was doing."

"Glad to know I'm not the only one that started that way," you say.

"It was overgrown and pitiful looking; difficult to stand anywhere without getting thorn scratches. One day I was standing there looking around, trying to figure out what I was going to do with the terrible mess, and Gary passed by. We were much younger then."

"'Wow, you are working hard, I see,' Gary said. He seemed impressed with my willingness to be out in the hot sun. I smiled with pride. I was about to respond, but I noticed him looking down at the tangled mess of thorns. 'What are you *trying* to grow here?'

"'I— uh.' I stammered. 'I planted a fruit tree.' He just humphed as if he didn't believe me.

"'Doesn't really look like you know what you're doing.'

"'Well,' I said. 'I'm just prepping the— I have to get the soil to— It's all about the— You wouldn't understand.'

"'I understand a mess when I see one.'

"'Dad-gum-it Gary, you old gossip. Get out of here,' I said as mean as a junkyard cat.

"'Ok, well, good luck with that,' that old gossip said as he went on his way. I was so embarrassed. I didn't ever want to be humiliated like that again. So I went directly to the lumber store and bought a truckload of wood. By the time the sun set, I had a six-foot fence around my entire garden. I went to bed satisfied with my work. The next morning I headed out to the now fenced garden. As I was standing in the thorn patch, I heard the voices of two neighbors passing by.

"'Oh, wow, a new fence,' I heard one say. It was Peggy with her walking partner, Marsha, from around the corner. They didn't know I was hiding behind my wooden privacy barricade. Marsha spoke up.

"'Well, I heard Gary say that it's nothing but a bunch of weeds back there behind that fence.' I was so mad I could have spit. Gary was ruining my reputation with the neighbors. I liked Peggy and Marsha, so I had to act.

"I started to grunt, moan, and yelp. I made the kind of sounds a person makes when they're working really hard in a garden. 'Sheesh, this gardening is hard work,' I said loud enough to be heard.

"'Hey there, neighbor,' Peggy called out over the fence. She and Marsha craned their necks to peer over the top boards. They could see me, but they couldn't see the garden below, and it was a good thing too because it was as wild as treasure island. I waved but then busied myself with more movement and noise, throwing leaves, twigs, and debris about like a wood chipper. After another round of hard-working grunts, Peggy and Marsha moved on, talking amongst themselves.

"'Wow, she's really giving it the ole' heave-ho, isn't she?' Peggy said.

"'I can't wait to see what comes out of that garden,' Marsha said. I could see that the fence was well worth the price, but her last comment concerned me.

"Day after day, I made sure that any neighbor who passed by, especially Gary, heard me grunting in the garden. When I exited my mystery garden each day, I made sure to be covered in soil and sweat. The entire neighborhood was very impressed with my diligence and tenacity. They had no idea of the wilderness that lurked behind those fence boards.

"'When are we going to get a taste of that fruit,' Peggy asked over the fence one sunny morning. I panicked. Outside the fence, my reputation had flourished. Behind the fence, the garden was nothing more than vines, thorns, and rocks. Buried deep among the thorns, there was a sapling I had planted the previous season, but I would be mortified to admit that the garden had not produced a single edible item.

"'I'm too busy to talk,' I said from behind my fence. 'I have to keep this garden in shape, and it takes all my time.

"'Come on, just one taste,' Peggy persisted.

"'I don't have time for all that,' I said again with a rise in my voice.

"'Loola, I'm coming in, ready or not.' Peggy said as playful as a songbird. I liked Peggy, which was why it hurt so bad to do what I did next. As she grabbed the handle of the gate, I jumped up with a fright and gripped the other side for all I was worth.

"I stood and glared at Peggy with a look that could'a boiled brass. Barely able to see her over the fence posts, I knew I had to make a full offensive. My reputation was at stake, and I couldn't stand to see it ruined. If Peggy got through that gate, everyone would know that my garden was a lie.

"'You lazy bum,' I said to Peggy. Though all I could see was her eyes, I knew I had stabbed her deep. I went on, 'You want to eat my fruit, but you haven't worked a single day in your own garden. Gary told me you don't even have a garden.' A tear rolled down her cheek. 'Get out of here, you nosy snoot,' I screamed.

"Peggy darted off, not saying a word. I had not only forgotten my ultimate goal, but I had swapped it out for an inferior one. My ultimate goal was to protect my fragile reputation. I wanted the approval of my neighbors so much more than I wanted fruit. I had to maintain the appearance that I was a hard-working gardener."

"Is that story true," you ask when Aunt Loola finally gets quiet. The hum of the road is all you can hear for a few long seconds.

"It's what I call a truthy story," Loola says.

"What does that mean?"

"It's a story that teaches a truth, but it's not a *true story* in the strictest sense," she admits.

"Well then, what are you trying to teach me?" you ask.

"Even when you know the ultimate goal, sometimes it's

tempting to swap it out for a different one. But every time you do, it causes problems."

"So, did you ever apologize to Peggy?" you ask.

"Well, that's the beauty of a truthy story; you get the lesson for free with none of the consequences."

"I see," you say.

"This is our exit, Honey," Loola says. You pull the car off the interstate expectant for your next truthy adventure.

22

DON'T SWAP

Do you realize that many Christians are in this situation? There are loads of believers who have replaced the ultimate goal of the Christian life with *maintaining a spiritual reputation*. There are likely millions who go through the motions, doing spiritual tasks, in order to get applause, approval, or accolades from others. There are countless that live out the Christian life in order to gain personal superiority. It's easy to fall into the trap of being self-righteous. I've been there, and I often realize that I need to climb out of that pit once again.

Whether it's simply approval or spiritual superiority, these are powerful motivations that drive many to stay in church, read their Bible, and pray. However, if you make approval and applause your ultimate goal, you will be heading down a dark and dangerous path. You'll have to put up fences and drive people away when they invite you to be vulnerable.

Have you ever known the lady that's prideful about her Bible Knowledge? She likes to make you feel small by quoting long memorized passages to you. Have you ever known the guy that pressures you to be at church every Sunday as he reminds you that he hasn't missed a service in forty years? Have you ever been cornered by the wild-eyed person who can't wait to tell you what God has been telling her in her all-night prayer sessions? I have. I know a lot of them. These folks drive me nuts.

In the last chapter, we talked about how Paul said, *the mindset of the flesh is death.*[1] A *mindset of the flesh* sounds like those frat-boy party-hounds we all knew in college. We usually think of the super-sinners when we hear the term *carnally minded,* which is what one translation calls the *mindset of the flesh.* Here's a surprising twist. The *mindset of the flesh* can be present in the condescending church lady just as much as the frat-boy.

When Paul says a *mindset of the flesh,* most people assume he's talking about thinking about gratuitous sin. However, that was not the only thing Paul had in mind. Paul was explaining that he had been attempting to accomplish righteousness by flesh-powered means.

Have you ever heard someone say, "It's possible to do *good* but to do it in my own strength?" That statement has bothered me for a long time because when I ask the person who said it, "What do you mean by that?" They will often say, "Oh, you know, when you do something *good,* but you're doing it for selfish motives." But that means that it's not *good.* Something that looks good but is motivated by selfish reasons is a sin. It seems to me that we use the term *doing good in my own strength* when we should just be honest and call it *sin.*

Jesus didn't like that kind of approach. To a group of people who had bad motives for doing what looked like *good* deeds, He said, You are like tombs that are painted white. Outside they look fine, but inside they are full of dead people's bones and all kinds of filth.[2]

A so-called *good deed* motivated by jealousy is a sin. Now, the deed itself might help someone else, but Jesus says that if you do good deeds so that you can get noticed, then it's hypocrisy, and he's not going to reward you for that kind of action.

It's easy to fall into the trap of doing *good* so that we get people's approval, applause, or praise. Jesus has a simple solution for this. Do your good deeds secretly. Give anonymously. Pray privately. Fast quietly. Donations, prayer, and fasting should be done privately to avoid the possibility of false motives. To add to this great advice, he says that God will reward people who do good things anonymously.[3]

I used to play in a rock band. Plenty of people wanted to get in a band so they could get on stage. There were a lot fewer people who wanted to run the sound mixer at the back of the room. Why? Both jobs are important. For one of those jobs, you get applause, and the other, you don't. I think that there is something similar that happens for Christians. It's easier to find someone to volunteer for the praise team than it is to find someone to volunteer to clean the toilets. This is why churches usually pay a custodian while having a line of volunteers waiting to get into the band. It's hard to think that this might not be pride at work.

Good deeds motivated by false motives are done with a *mindset of the flesh*. Pride is a fleshly motivation. Jealousy is a fleshly motivation. The sin of false motives is so insidious it often seems to go unnoticed by those who are experiencing it. It is sin, nonetheless. This is why a person can be living with a *mindset of the flesh* while doing lots of Christian tasks. An elder, a deacon, a minister, or a choir leader can all be living in a mindset of the flesh.

The *mindset of the flesh* is death. How can you know if you are in a flesh-powered mindset or not? Well, look at the fruit that your habits produce. Paul tells us what the fruits of the flesh are,[4] and they aren't pretty. If your habits are producing pride, jealousy, bitterness, dissension, anger, or others, then maybe it's time to reexamine your ultimate goal in doing those tasks.

Do you pray, attend church, or read your Bible for approval from others? If so, you've replaced God's ultimate goal for your life with an artificial goal of your own. It's so important that you strive for God's ultimate goal for your life. You can't do it with the *try harder, the do more or the self-serving* mentality. All of those are the *mindset of the flesh.* They are a dead-end road. You're going to need a fresh approach.

Let's review the ultimate goal of your Christian life. The goal of your garden isn't to supply you with secrecy and pride. It is to bear sweet life-sustaining fruit. The main purpose of your remaining time is to have abundant life. We'll talk about how to accomplish that in a while, but first, let's take a look at another of the most common gardening mistakes.

23
ESCAPE

You put the car in park in front of an old, dilapidated-looking house. It could be the scene of a blockbuster horror film. There are holes in the roof. Wood rot marks the siding. The door hangs askew. Despite the horrid state of the untenable home, you notice a garden that fills the entire front yard.

"Are you sure this is it?" you ask.

“It’s the right place.”

“The right place, if you want to get murdered,” you mumble. Aunt Loola climbs out of the car and begins, cane in hand, toward the front door. You unbuckle and follow reluctantly behind her.

As you approach the sprawling garden that stretches across the otherwise overgrown property, you notice that the well-kept plot is filled with plant life not so different from what fills your own garden with one obvious distinction. The ivy, vines, and thistles are laid out in perfect, well-ordered rows.

"Why would someone intentionally raise bull nettle?" you

ask as you spot the alien-looking plant, known for the itchy sting it inflicts on contact.

"I'll let him tell you," Aunt Loola says as she climbs the front porch steps and knocks on the door. "Cravis," she calls between incessant knocks. "It's me, Loola."

"Cravis," you whisper. "What kind of name is that?"

"Loola, is that really you?" A gruff voice rumbles from somewhere deep within the bowels of the house. The creaking of the rotten floor precedes the appearance of an ancient man with a beard that covers his belly. He looks like he could be cast in a fantasy film. This is not least in part because he's holding a mortar and pestle, stained with the crimson juice of some recent project.

Before saying anything, Cravis dips his thumb into the red potion he's holding and wipes it across Aunt Loola's forehead.

"Cravis," Aunt Loola whines in protest.

"It's an elixir I've been working on," the old man says through a white beard tinted with red-stained fringes. "It keeps the bad jinxes away."

Loola pulls a handkerchief from her pocket and removes the red from her forehead. She turns to you and motions with a sweeping gesture toward the strange character. "Cravis T. Hollowbody," Loola says as she steps out of the way.

Cravis raises a hand and begins moving toward you. At first, it looks as if he wants to shake, but his red-soaked thumb hints otherwise.

"None, for me, thanks," you say, putting both hands in front of your face. He reaches through anyway and marks your forehead with the inky stuff. It smells like pulverized foliage left to putrify in swamp water. You wipe it away with the back of your hand.

"Cravis," Aunt Loola calls a little louder than would be

needed for average human ears. “I wanted you to show my friend your garden.”

“Garden?” Cravis says, turning on the woman. “It’s not a garden,” now turning back to you with his deep yellowy eyes. “It’s a pharmacy, a doctor’s office, a hospital, even.”

“What do you mean?" you ask, a little frightened to engage.

"Well, take this one, for instance," Cravis says. He steps over a row of three-leaf ivy and stands above a tall line of prickly spikes. As he raises his voice to a volume worthy of an oratorio, Aunt Loola steps beside you.

“Here we go,” she whispers so that Cravis can’t hear. She smiles as if you are in for a show.

"Blister bean porantila," Cravis bellows as he plucks a strange bud from a spire of hideous green daggers. The flora appears as if it could sever a finger. Loola leans in close.

"That's not really what it's called," she says. Cravis continues, unaware of the whispered commentary.

"Porantila, grants you the voice of the Arcon," he says as wild-eyed as a cat in a burning house. "Take one of these, and whatever you speak with sincerity will come true. Here, try one,” he says.

"No, that's ok," you say firmly. Loola declines as well, so Cravis opens his mouth, throws back his head, and swallows the green sallow bean whole.

"Good fortune shall come to me today. Thus, I declare it," Cravis chants in a sing-song voice. Coming out of the trance, he says, "Eww, I'll feel that one in a little while," placing a hand on his rotund belly. "It usually induces vomiting within a few hours. Oh what about Sagulus gargantuan?"

"Also, a made-up name," Loola whispers.

“Let’s say you have a fever, or a cough, or a bad hair day.”

He plucks a flower from a thorny tight-trimmed hedge. "Crush this up, make a warm tea from its petals, and—"

"Cravis, Honey, you're not actually consuming those, are you? They're poisonous!" Loola says.

"No, of course not. I make it into tea and soak my shirt in it before I put it on. It does wonders! I haven't had to take an aspirin in years."

On and on he goes. His garden contains what he calls thine-cloves for infections, snooderberries for rashes, and slarg for headaches. He even has a plant he calls golden listrup that supposedly cures financial trouble.

After ten minutes of rambling about the relative benefits of salustrictus, a plant that looks amazingly similar to dollar weed, which is supposed to fix bad posture, Loola speaks up.

"Well, thanks for letting us visit, Cravis," she says.

"Going so soon?" Cravis grumbles. "I haven't shown you my constrictus vines." It takes another few minutes before you are both in the car and driving away.

"What in the world!" You nearly shout as if you've been holding your breath for an hour. "Was any of that true?"

"Not a stitch, Honey," Aunt Loola says.

"Why did you bring me here?"

"Cautionary tale," she explains.

"Has he lost his mind?"

"No, not at all," she says. "He's actually quite brilliant. He was a medical doctor for about two decades before he got into gardening and fell for one of the classic blunders."

"Which is?"

"He believes that he should be able to evade all suffering. He thinks he can escape every problem that life throws at him, and he's convinced the key to dodging all pain and difficulty is in those magic plants."

"His goal for gardening is different," you say.

"That's right. He's trying to escape trouble with what grows." Loola says as you turn the car onto the highway and head home.

24
ESCAPE ARTISTS

God has a big important goal for your Christian life. However, there are those who have substituted God's goal for a goal of their own. In the last chapter, we talked about substituting pride for God's ultimate goal. In this chapter, we'll talk about another substitution. I call those who do this swap the *Christian Escape Artists.*

Like a faith-based Houdini, they seem to believe that they can get out of any tight jam with only their faith. The *Christian Escape Artists* believe that Christianity is a means for escaping life's difficulties. In their opinion, no Christian should have to experience pain, financial distress, or sickness. Provided that there is enough faith, each person can supposedly escape these uncomfortable aspects of life.

There is a strong emphasis on the Spirit among *Christian Escape Artists.* However, it seems that they are often begging the Spirit for things the Spirit is not currently offering. It's kind of like ordering a Big Mac at Taco Bell; it's not on the menu. If a healing or financial deliverance isn't on the Spirit's menu, it doesn't matter how long you stand there and argue; it ain't happenin'.

I think the ridiculous nature of these *Escape Artists* was clearly revealed by the Covid Quarantine of 2020. Churches all over the country closed their doors for a time. At that painful moment in our history, we could have really used some people with the gift of healing. We could have very much benefited from some financial deliverance. Not surprisingly, the churches of those famous faith healers closed their doors with the rest of us. No doubt, they had some lofty-sounding rationalization for discontinuing services. In the end, they did what they believed in. They *escaped* the public in fear of disease, the very thing they claim to have power over. My dad has often said, "why don't the faith healers go visit the hospitals? There are lots of sick people wanting to get better there."

It's true that early in the church, the Spirit was using apostles to physically heal. Jesus Himself healed many. However, these miracles had a very specific purpose. Jesus' miracles were performed to prove that He was telling the truth about His identity and purpose.[1] The Apostles were allowed to do miracles to prove they were speaking the truth about Jesus' identity and purpose.[2] A reading of the New Testament doesn't turn up a single miracle that is performed only for the purpose of *escaping* trouble. The purpose of miracles is to authenticate the speaker so that people who witness the miracle can believe.

In reality, Jesus and the Apostles rarely escaped trouble. The Apostles left their livelihoods and lived with few to no worldly possessions. Jesus was homeless. John ended his life in exile away from everyone he loved. The rest of the Apostles were brutally murdered for their faith. Even Jesus was killed in the worst way possible after experiencing all kinds of pain and suffering. If the purpose of the Christian life was to *escape* pain, suffering, and financial ruin, then all the disciples and even Jesus Himself failed miserably.

The purpose of the Christian life is not to *escape* suffering. Instead, Christians should expect it. I'll let Paul explain. To his star student, Timothy, he once said, *all who want to live a godly life in Christ Jesus will be persecuted.*[3]

Don't miss this! Paul says this is a fundamental rule to trying to live a godly life. You will be persecuted. You will face trouble, affliction, suffering, and pain. The pain we feel may not always seem connected to our being Christians, but don't forget what Jesus said. He broached the topic long before Paul wrote his letter to his buddy Tim.

Jesus said, *in this world, you will have trouble.*[4] This might force a sprout of chill bumps down your arms. You can hear the ominous music in the background, right? Trouble is coming, and it will find you. Not everyone will experience the same suffering, but you can rest assured that it is going to come around sooner or later. In his gospel, John talks about a group of people who were believers but tried to avoid the trouble that accompanies being a Christian.

John said, *many did believe in him [Jesus] even among the rulers, but because of the Pharisees, they did not confess Him so that they would not be banned from the synagogue.*[5] This group wanted to avoid all of the consequences of being open followers of Christ. So what did they do? They stayed quiet about their newfound faith in Jesus. Unfortunately, pretending you aren't a Christian won't keep you out of trouble either, because as Paul said, *the wrath of God is being revealed from heaven against all... who suppress the truth.*[6] Trying to suppress the truth about God, even the truth that you've believed, isn't going to keep you from experiencing trouble. That's because God will discipline those he loves.[7]

This is an inescapable fact: If you're a Christian, whether

you are trying to live a godly life or living an ungodly life, you will experience trouble, suffering, pain, and affliction. Suffering may come from things that don't relate to our faith. However, as soon as suffering comes, we are immediately thrown into a spiritual battle.

I once had my cornea scratched by my then three-year-old. It was the worst pain I've ever felt. In the moments when the agony was the worst, you can bet I was talking to Jesus. My prayers were the most fervent they have ever been in my life. Suffering, even suffering that seems unconnected to spiritual matters, is always an opportunity to set our minds on the spiritual.

One of the biggest questions that I get, especially when I'm talking to people who have turned their back on the faith, is *Why does God let bad things happen to good people?* The answer that the Bible gives to that question is often unsatisfying for unbelievers, but for us who are saved, it can be downright exciting.

For example, let's look at what Paul said about suffering. He explained, *we rejoice in our sufferings, knowing that suffering produces endurance. perseverance, character; and character, hope.*[8]

Those who understand the purpose of suffering can actually rejoice when they feel the pain. When we face suffering gladly, it produces endurance. This means we grow spiritually stronger when we face afflictions. That spiritual endurance results in character. As you face suffering and face it with a spiritual mindset, it's like a fast-track character-building program. He explains that character results in hope. He concludes the train of thought by showing that hope makes us eager for the Lord to return. In other words, it sets our minds on Spiritual things.

Facing suffering with a kind of gladness produces this amazing cycle in us. Ultimately it drives us toward a godly mindset which results in a more abundant life. Imagine being able to experience love, peace, and even joy in the middle of suffering. That's a truly abundant life.

James, the half brother of Jesus, said, *Consider it a great joy, my brothers and sisters, whenever you experience various trials because you know that the testing of your faith produces endurance. And let endurance have its full effect so that you may be mature and complete, lacking nothing.*[9]

Notice that James doesn't say you can get to the point where you *lack nothing* by easy living. Your process of maturing is going to require some trials and pains. His imperative instruction is that we keep in mind the amazing outcome of considering our trials as a gift from God.

Suffering needs a rebranding campaign. For years I virtually plugged up my ears when I heard teachers talking about suffering because I didn't want to grow that way. I wanted to grow, but I was hoping there was a kind of premium package that allowed me to avoid the rough stuff. I was doing the opposite of what James says to do in these verses, and so too are all the Christian *escape artists.* He instructs us to rebrand our suffering as joy.

Even Peter got in on this discussion when he said, *you rejoice in this, even though now for a short time, if necessary, you suffer grief in various trials.*[10]

The ultimate goal of the Christian life is not to be a person who escape*s* suffering. Instead, our goal is to have abundant life, even in the midst of suffering. It turns out that suffering is one of the best tools to allow us to move toward that abundant life. Don't fall into the classic blunder of thinking the goal of your Christian life is to *escape* trouble. Embrace trouble with joy as you set your mind on Spiritual things. That will bring about the abundant life you need.

25

TREES WITH BAD FRUIT

As you drive toward home, you and Aunt Loola continue to talk about Cravis and his strange garden.

"How did you get to know him?" you ask.

"We used to be—" Aunt Loola pauses. It's rare for her to be at a loss for words. "Cravis and I used to be very close."

"Really?"

"This was before you were born. I had taken a liking to him. I would bring him fresh produce, and we'd sit out under the summer stars and talk late into the night. I shared my love for all things botanical with him. I even convinced him to start his own garden. Before long, he had planted a row of berry bushes."

"Oh, so his garden wasn't always packed with bull nettle?" you ask.

"It might as well have been," Loola says. "I had only been gardening a few years at that time, and so I didn't recognize the plant he had sown. No fruit had sprouted yet, so he pointed at the leaves of the little bushes. He said the bush was a blueberry bush."

"Was that true?"

"Well, it did look like a blueberry bush, but I'd been gardening long enough to know that you judge a tree by its fruit, not by its leaves and stem. I mean, there are a few things you can check, like if the sap is milky or the stem is bitter, but you never know until you can see the fruit."

"Did you explain that?"

"Honey, there ain't no explaining nothing to that man. I did try, but he wouldn't listen. He just kept talking about how magical gardening was."

"I'm guessing they weren't blueberries," you say.

"Good guess. When the bush finally did start sprouting, the berries were red and hung in tight clusters."

"Is that bad?"

"Only about half of red berries are edible, and a lot of times clustered berries are not good."

"So what happened?"

"I got this call from Cravis one afternoon. He was practically hyperventilating. He was going on and on about the amazing benefits of the berries he was growing. He said he saw visions. I knew that there was a problem, so I grabbed my plant identification book, hoped in the car, and went over right away.

"When I got there, the first thing I saw was the visitors. There were a half dozen people in his garden. Cravis was plucking berries and handing them out to his neighbors. They were eating them by the handful."

"Oh, no," you say.

"Yeah, no kidding. Before I knew it, Cravis was trying to cram these bright red BBs in my mouth. I had to fight him off. He was telling me about the spiritual visions he was having after every bite."

"Spiritual visions?" you ask.

"Well, I knew right away what that meant. Some toxic berries make you hallucinate."

"Oh my," you respond. "He was eating toxic berries?"

"Not just eating them, but passing them out to his friends. I started trying to figure out how many people he had given the berries to, their names, and where they lived."

"Why?" you ask.

"Because a berry that makes you hallucinate isn't to be messed around with. I needed to let them know they had been poisoned and that they should see a doctor immediately. I plucked a handful, and laid my Edible Plants handbook on the hood of my car, and went to work. It didn't take long to find the crimson devils. Sure enough, he was eating and handing out little red poison pills."

"Did anyone die?" you ask.

"Thankfully, no. They cause intense vomiting. Almost everyone stopped eating them right away."

"Almost everyone?" you ask. "Who would eat them after that?"

"Cravis T. Hollowbody, that's who. He convinced a few others too. He taught a few of his gardening disciples that if they ate only one at a time, then they could still get the hallucinogenic effect. Of course, even one will make you throw up, but as he put it, 'a little tummy trouble is worth the spiritual revelations.'"

"Are you serious?" you ask.

"Yep. We had a big fight over it, of course. Now he's moved on to much more extravagant lunacy, as you saw."

"It's amazing he hasn't poisoned himself to death or killed someone else," you say as you turn the car onto Loola's street. "Why didn't people see through him? I mean, he was poisoning them. Why did they keep coming back for more?"

"I don't know. Some people just want to be fooled, I guess," Aunt Loola says.

"You're like a botanical superhero, you know," you say.

"I prefer garden ninja," she says with a giggle. "Though, there is a lesson in all this. You know what it is?"

"I'm about to; I think," you say.

"You can tell what's safe by examining the fruit. If any of Cravis' poor neighbors knew how to identify poison berries, then they would have saved themselves from a lot of vomiting. You got to look at the fruit."

"Look at the fruit," you repeat as you pull up in front of Aunt Loola's house.

26
ROTTEN FRUIT TEACHERS

Do you have a *personal* Bible? If you do, you are unique in comparison to most people in Christian history. It wasn't until late, possibly the turn of the last century, that the practice of having a *personal* Bible arrived. Despite the fact that most of Christian History didn't even have a concept of the *personally* owned Bible, the Apostles still expected Christians to take in God's word in some way. It isn't until modern history that someone could learn from the Word of God in private isolation. A person can take their own Bible and go try to figure it out alone.

In talking about some of the portions of the Bible which Paul wrote, Peter once said, "Paul has written to you according to the wisdom given to him… in all his letters. There are some things hard to understand in them. Untaught and unstable people will twist them to their own destruction, as they also do with the rest of the Scriptures.[1]

Do you realize that you might be doing something dangerous when you study your own *personal* Bible all by yourself? The Bible is for everyone, but there are things in the

Bible that are hard to understand. To complicate things, no amount of mere human intelligence makes it possible to grasp what's in the Bible. There are things in the Bible that untaught people will twist. There is a danger in trying to understand the Bible alone. It's for this reason that I believe Scripture is intended to be studied together in a community of other trustworthy believers. It works best when we are being taught by reliable teachers and constantly praying for wisdom.

I'm reminded of a friend who became a believer when we were in high school. A few times, we got together to study the Bible. There were things that were obvious to me, probably because I had been taught by others. However, they were anything but obvious to him. I remember asking some questions about a verse that seemed to be as clear as the nose on my face. His answer made me crinkle that nose and look back at the verse. Were we talking about the same line? We need to be praying for understanding and wisdom, and we need teachers to teach us. However, choosing a trustworthy teacher comes with some serious risks.

I think that's why Paul said to his star student, Timothy, *what you have heard from me in the presence of many witnesses, commit to faithful men who will be able to teach others also.*[2] Notice that Paul taught in the presence of *many witnesses.* He didn't conduct backroom, secret society meetings. He taught where multiple people could hear, check, and verify what he was saying. In addition to that, the teaching of God's word wasn't to be entrusted to just anyone. The continuation of Paul's teaching was to be committed to *faithful* men.

If you are beginning to study God's word for the first time, or if you have been learning from the Bible for years, consider who you're listening to. Are they reliable? Are they committed to teaching God's word accurately? Do they listen to others and teach in accordance with other *witnesses,* who also understand God's word.

Jesus warned that there would be false teachers who might lead you astray. He said, *beware of false prophets, who come to you in sheep's clothing, but inwardly they are ravenous wolves... by their fruits you will know them.*[3] Fortunately, while it is true that we can be led astray, Jesus explains that we are not without hope. We are able to identify false teachers. How? We can identify false teachers by their fruit.

Many have thought that this means we will be able to tell if someone is a false teacher by how they act, but that can't be right. Remember, they have come *in sheep's clothing.* They are wolves who wear wool. They have come playing the part. They act right on the outside. They put on a good show. They look like they are righteous. When Jesus talks about their *fruit,* He must mean something else. What is the fruit of a teacher?

The fruit that Jesus is talking about is the fruit of their mouth. He says, *for a tree is known by its fruit... out of the abundance of the heart the mouth speaks.*[4] It's a Bible teacher's words that we have to judge them by. You can recognize a false prophet by what he teaches. It means we better be listening closely.

It may seem overwhelming to try and discern a false teacher, but you have a tool that can help you determine who is reliable. For so many centuries, people simply trusted what the preacher, pastor, or parishioner said because copies of Scripture were hard to get ahold of. However, since so many people have a *personal* Bible today, the average person is able and responsible to consider the reliability of Bible teachers based on what they know of God's word.

I like how Luke puts it. He explains that when Paul went to Thessalonica, the people didn't accept his teaching. However, when he arrived in Beria, the people were eager to hear him, but they didn't just trust him without verification. Luke says, *these were more fair-minded than those in Thessalonica, in that they received the word with all readiness, and searched the Scriptures daily to find out whether these things were so.*[5]

Even though Paul's message was accompanied by miracles, they didn't just listen and swallow anything they were taught by Him. They took their own responsibility seriously. They would have had a handwritten copy of the Old Testament in the synagogue. It wasn't easy to get it out, and it was extremely valuable. Nonetheless, they went to the trouble of checking what Paul was teaching against their copy of the Torah. That's how they determined that he was trustworthy.

One of the marks of a false teacher is a person who teaches that salvation comes by doing good deeds. You can see it in Jesus' discussion about the false teachers who are *wolves in sheep's clothing.* He says that when those false teachers stand before the Lord, they will claim their good works make them worthy of salvation. They will say, *have we not prophesied in Your name, cast out demons in Your name, and done many wonders in Your name?*[6] Jesus's silence on their question is deafening. He doesn't acknowledge that what they did were good works. Instead, he explains that what they did was evil. They are then denied entrance into Heaven.[7] Those who believe and teach that salvation comes by doing good works will be denied entrance.

The sad aspect of Jesus' story is that those false teachers won't arrive alone. They will have a line behind them who have listened to them. Jesus makes it clear that each person has a responsibility to check what they are taught against Scripture. Don't be lead astray by a false teacher; it will mean that what you're growing isn't fruit. It could result, at the least, in a lack of abundant life. For many, though, the stakes are even higher than that.

If you are going to be a Christian who learns from God's word, you are going to need to pray for understanding, and study scripture as part of a community of faith, but also you will have to consider the teachers you listen to. In that pursuit, you must check what Bible teachers say against God's word.

There are thousands of false teachers throughout the world who are regularly robbing Christians of their abundant life and even their assurance of eternal life. If you've found yourself under the teaching of someone that regularly stirs up something other than love, joy, peace, patience, kindness, and the like, then it might be worth examining his or her teaching a little closer. When God's word is taught responsibly, the ultimate result will line up with your ultimate goal, which is abundant life.

27

GARDEN HARDER

"I'm going to church. Do you want to come?" Aunt Loola says over the phone early Sunday morning. You're beginning to expect calls and visits before the sun is up, but you're a little nervous about her invitation.

"I'm not sure that—"

"I want you to hear what Preacher has to say. He told me he was going to tell a gardening story."

"Like, gardening advice?"

"No, probably not," she says. "More like a parable, I think."

Not long after this conversation, you find yourself sitting in a wooden pew. You're one of only a handful of members of the local congregation present. A woman with a large hair-do manages to play a piano song that features the most out-of-tune section of the keyboard. She's followed by a man in a suit who walks confidently to the front of the room.

Loola leans over and says, "That's The Reverend-Pastor, Brother Dudley Lionel Graves."

"Why does he have so many names?" you whisper.

"Hush, and listen, Honey."

He takes his place behind the oversized wooden pulpit and begins to speak.

"There once was a man who planted a vineyard. After many months be began to see that his fruit vines were not producing any fruit. Thorns, rocks, weeds, and dry ground surrounded the poor fruit shoots. It seemed hopeless. He began to panic, but he refused to give up. He was determined, committed, insistent on *making* that vine grow fruit. He said, 'I'll just have to try harder?'

"He had an idea. To get the vines healthy, they needed some exercise. Each morning he would limber them up by stretching them back and forth. He would then take each sprig, shoot, and shaft and force them through an exercise routine. Not only did the vines need his help to do the exercises, they still refused to produce fruit. 'I'll just have to try harder.'

"He had an idea. 'Exercise is better with music.' He started using music in the morning sessions, but not just any music. He only allowed *gardening* songs to play over the vineyard's loudspeaker. 'Sing along now,' he said to the vines. Even with the music and the forced movement, the plants were stubborn. They refused to grow fruit. 'I'll have to try harder,' he said.

"He had an idea. 'These vines need knowledge. They need to see what they are supposed to do.' Adding to the routine, the vinedresser laid out articles from gardening magazines in front of the vines. 'Study these, every day, and you'll become good vines.' No matter how much he tried, the vines were stubborn. 'I'll have to try harder,' he said.

"He had an idea. 'These vines need some motivation,' he said. A little fear is enough to get them to produce. To the morning routine, the man added a mantra. "Repeat after me," he said. "If I don't produce some fruit, I'll be torn up from the root." Over and over, he chanted the frightening phrase. And wouldn't you know it, those vines remained as stubborn as ever.

You continue to listen as the preacher develops his parable. Before long, your mind wanders, and you find yourself thinking of your own garden. As you allow yourself to get lost in the daydream, you're surprised to discover Aunt Loola tugging on your arm.

"You going to stay here all day?"

"Oh, sorry," you say. "I kind of spaced out."

"What did you think of the sermon?" she asks.

"I liked it," you say as you help her to her feet. "I'm still thinking about that vineyard story."

"Yeah, I thought that probably got your attention."

"I'm not sure if I quite understand the point," you say as you follow Loola out of the pew and toward the back of the church. She greets some other congregants briefly as you step into the midday sun.

"You did space out," Loola says. "He explained the meaning of the story. I guess you missed that part?"

"Oh, really." You smile shyly as you reach for your keys. You open the door for Loola and she gets into the car. Loola is talking as soon as you get into the driver's seat.

"The vine man could fill up all his time doing more, but if it's not what the vines need for growing, then it's just wasted time. There's a lot of folks that think they just need to try harder and do more. Trying harder don't make no difference if the *more* you're trying ain't what's needed."

"Ok. I guess that makes sense," you say.

"Course, his stories always make sense."

"But how does a gardener figure out what is needed," you say.

"Well, if they're smart, then they just need to ask sweet ole' Aunt Loola, and they'll be just fine," she says.

"Back home?" you ask as you pull out of the parking lot.

"No," she says. "Haven't you ever been to church before?"

"I— uh—"

"We're not done till the fat lady eats," Loola says with a laugh. "Since you were my visitor at church, you get to pick where we do lunch. You can pick from all of the cafeterias in town with a buffet and free refills."

"There's only one," you reply.

"Like I said, you get to pick."

28
TRY HARDER

Many Christians believe that it is determination, willpower, and commitment that will force their spiritual life to grow and to eventually bear fruit. They do the *try harder* method; the *do more* approach. They pile up all kinds of tasks that seem good but don't bring about growth.

Have you ever been there? Week after week, you hear sermons that corroborate this mentality. You are bombarded by messages that tell you that you're not committed enough. You hear preachers and friends that make you feel as if your determination is too weak. You begin to repeat the refrain to yourself, believing that you just have to give it more *effort.*

So you try. You try. And you try again. Each time you get more demoralized. You get more discouraged. You feel as if the entire Christian life is a series of funhouse mirrors. Every so often, you hear a powerful message from a talented speaker who encourages you to dig deeper, and you do, for a day, a week, maybe even a year. At the end of it, you always wind up in the same place. No matter how hard you try, it isn't enough. You can't make yourself grow spiritually. You keep stacking up the *do-gooder* habits. You keep agreeing to *do more* Christian tasks, but your best efforts seem about as effective as a pile of rocks.

It reminds me of that story from the gospels about Martha and Mary. Martha invited Jesus to her house. Martha's sister, Mary, was there. Instead of helping Martha host their guests, Mary just plopped down at Jesus' feet and listened to him teach. Martha, being the hospitable housekeeper, was busy doing all the stuff that a good host does. She was annoyed that sister Mary wasn't helping. So Martha tried to get Jesus to side with her. Martha asked Jesus to tell Mary to get up and help her. Jesus has this amazing response.

Jesus said, *Martha, Martha, you are getting worried and upset about too many things. Only one thing is important. Mary has made the right choice, and it will never be taken away from her.*[1] Both Martha and Mary were believers. They both were considered Jesus' friends as well. Martha was busy with Christian activity. What could be more *Christian* than preparing a meal for Jesus and his disciples? Nonetheless, Martha fell into the trap of *Christian busy work*, while Mary was willing to drop some of the normal responsibilities in order to do the more important task.

The story with Martha and Mary is a reminder that Jesus isn't trying to simply engage us in an endless parade of empty and meaningless tasks. He has a point. He has a purpose. He has an ultimate goal for your life. His goal for your life is clear and easy to understand. He wants you to have abundant life.

Are you a Martha? Do you find yourself trying to do it all? Have you been a *try harder*, Christian? Have you fallen into the *do more* trap only to discover that it doesn't do you any good? Is it possible that all of those Christian activities are actually getting in the way? Your mission is to be transformed by your new mindset, not to be constantly engaged in busy work. In the next section we'll look at another aspect that often gets in the way of abundant life.

29
THORN FARMER

"So, when are we going to start working on my garden?" you ask.

"Are you sure you're ready?" Aunt Loola asks as she sets her tray down on the table. The line at the buffet was long, and your stomach is growling.

"Yeah, I'm ready. Why wouldn't I be?" you say as you set your own plate down and take a seat across from her. The only buffet-style cafeteria in town, Lois's, is filled with Sunday afternoon lunch customers. She raises her voice over the din.

"I mean, are you sure the garden is worth your effort?" Loola asks. You're surprised at her words. *Is she experiencing a sudden drop in confidence, or maybe blood sugar?*

"Well, yeah," you venture, not sure where she's going with this.

"Ok, imagine this. You're standing in your garden months from now. You've put in a lot of work, but you're feeling frustrated by all of the weeds, thorns, and unwanted upgrowth."

"Well, that's not hard to imagine," you say as you take a bite of your lunch. Loola continues.

"Let's say that as you look around your overgrown garden, you start to wonder why you're so focused on fruit. After all, there are lots of things growing in the garden. There's clover, pigweed, and Canadian thistle. Sure, they're weeds but they provide an adequate green ground cover."

“I don’t want weeds. I want fruit!” you say between bites.

“Yeah, but it’s way easier to grow wild weed flowers,” Loola says with more pressure than she normally uses.

“Well, I— uh—” you pause. “Are you saying I should give up?”

“No, not completely. Maybe just lower your expectations. I mean, the fruit tree is fine. It will survive, even if it doesn’t grow any fruit. Maybe just focus on the weeds. After all, you’ve got ragwort and oxalis that both have an acceptable yellow flower. There’s some creeping thistle that buds with purple petals.”

“Those are considered weeds too, aren’t they?" you ask.

“Really, what’s the difference in the end? A plant is a plant is a plant.”

“Are you serious?" you ask.

"Weeds are way easier to cultivate." Aunt Loola says. "You hardly even need to water. They'll grow on their own. Before you know it, the garden will be filled with color." You've heard enough. You're starting to get frustrated.

"Listen," you say, leaning over the table. You can feel the warm flush filling your cheeks. "I don't know what's come over you, but I want fruit, not hogworts, oxe wheel weeds, or whatever you called them. I want fruit. I know I don't know what I'm doing, but I want fruit. You said you would help me. I'll gladly accept your help, but I'm going for fruit whether you help me or not."

“Are you sure?”

“Yes. I want fruit, abundant fruit," you say definitively.

Aunt Loola takes a drink of her tea as she eyes you for a long moment. A smile begins to creep across her face.

"Good, I think you're ready to start. We'll get to it Monday morning," Loola says.

"Oh— well—" you try to say. "Was that some kind of test?"

"Of course it was," Loola says.

"And I passed?"

"Just barely."

"Good." You take a drink from your cup now. Loola gives your hand a warm, matronly pat as she giggles gently.

"Sorry for being ornery," Loola says. You smile at her.

"I've come to expect at least a little harassment every day." You take a bite while still thinking about her strange approach to teaching. "Just out of curiosity. What would happen if I decided to cultivate the weeds?" She considers your question for a few seconds before she responds.

"Oh, it'd probably go well at first, but about the time you start to celebrate your ingenuity, things would begin to turn. The weedy plants would bud and flower, but with those flowers would come all kinds of new intruders. The new sprouts would bring bees, wasps, gnats, and flies. Creeping insects would begin to fill the ground, attracted to the new bouquet of options. An entirely new ecosystem would come to the buffet. To eat the insects, birds would arrive. Interested in bird eggs, squirrels, and other rodents would move in. Hoping to feast on the rodent population, snakes would take up residence. On it goes."

"So you're saying, I don't want the weeds?"

"You don't want weeds," she says. "Of course, the biggest problem would be that your fruit tree would never bear any fruit if you cultivated the weeds."

"And fruit is good, right?"

"Fruit is good. Especially peach, and at the moment, I'm craving some peach cobbler," Loola says as she lifts her empty plate and hands it to you. You rise with a smile and turn for the buffet. You're about to walk, but Loola stops you. "Honey, I don't eat peach cobbler alone." She grabs your plate and hands it to you as well. You skip off to fill your plates.

30

CULTIVATING SIN

One of the greatest detriments to the abundant life is when we feed and nurture the wrong aspects of our lives. Jesus illustrated this idea in his famous parable about various kinds of soils. In his parable, he said, *other seed fell among thorns, which grew up with it and choked the plants.*[1] He goes on to explain what the thorn-choked plants represent.

He said, *the seed that fell among thorns stands for those who hear [God's word], but as they go on their way, they are choked by life's worries, riches, and pleasures, and they do not mature.*[2]

Here Jesus explains that there are a number of believers who legitimately hear and believe the saving message. However, they will never reach full maturity. In their spiritual garden, thorny weeds are allowed to grow. Those thorns represent worries, riches, and pleasures. Certainly, there are worries, riches, and pleasures that are not sins, but Jesus shows that as certain things grow more prominent in our lives, they can choke out our spiritual growth.

The writer of Hebrews explains that it's easy for life to get filled with *sin that so easily entangles.*[3] One of the greatest hindrances to the Christian life is sin. I know, I know, it sounds old school, right? It sounds like I'm some kind of a pulpit-pounding preacher from the turn of the last century, but hear me out.

The problem with sin is where it leads. You can't do a single sin in isolation. Sin moves the person along a sliding path. James put it this way, *after desire has conceived, it gives birth to sin; and sin, when it is full-grown, gives birth to death.*[4] If you let your sin nature have complete control of your life, it will lead to death. Every sin is a gateway to a greater sin. That sin is a gateway to one more dangerous. That sin-paved road leads to your death if you don't stop it.

When I was in my early teens, I was introduced to porn by a friend. I didn't dabble all that much at first. Though, over time it grew from an unhealthy desire to a full-blown lust problem. At that time, the internet was coming of age, and free porn was suddenly readily available. By my twenties, I was pretty hooked; despite knowing it was bad, I fed and nurtured my habit. Eventually, my porn consumption began to transform the way I thought about things.

Although I couldn't recognize it at the time, the sin, which had originally stayed very confined to one part of my life, was beginning to branch out into other areas. My porn guilt pressured me to isolate myself from believers who were growing. To do that, I had to convince myself that they were hypocrites or two-faced. Thinking that led me to become bitter and cynical. That outlook affected how I viewed everyone.

I grew jealous and angry as I distanced myself from church. I stopped praying, for the most part. I didn't open my Bible very much because it usually made me feel guilty. All of this led to me doubting a whole host of things I had believed. I found myself questioning even the basics.

That singular sin that began in my early teens grew to a massive, unwieldy dark tree laden with black poison-fruit. Just like weeds, sin seeds and grows other sin. Often the sins that we find in our lives don't seem like they could be related to each other, but they are.

The author of Hebrews said that we must be careful because it's possible that you can *be deceived by sin and hardened against God.*[5] You may feel like your sin isn't affecting your Christian life, but if that's how you feel, you've already fallen prey to what this verse explains. Sin is a deceiver. It warps your mind in such a way that it will harden you toward God. I felt the hardening, due to my sin, in about a thousand ways.

One of the greatest mistakes we could make is avoiding the hard task of removing sin. As we will see in the following chapters, we don't fight sin directly.

After all, even the spiritual superhero Paul said, *I don't want to do what is wrong, but I do it anyway... when I want to do what is right, I inevitably do what is wrong... there is another power within me that is at war with my mind. This power makes me a slave to the sin that is still within me. Oh, what a miserable person I am! Who will free me from this life that is dominated by sin and death?*[6]

There was a time in Paul's life that he did the *try harder* method. What he found was that he couldn't make himself stop certain sins, just by willpower. He couldn't deliver himself from the cycle of dead living that he was experiencing. Instead, he began looking for a way out.

My kids are still learning to share. It's a tough lesson. It's a tough lesson because the sin nature doesn't like to share. In fact, it refuses. Sin wants total dominion. Paul said that if you let it sin will, "reign in your mortal body." Sin wants to rule you. If you don't put up a fight, it will.

Sin is clever, though. You may have thought you beat sin when you really only exchanged one sin for another. There are those who have fallen prey to the sin exchange program. What's that? you say. It's impossible to make the flesh stop sinning by using flesh-powered means. You can't just *try really hard* to stop sinning and succeed. However, the flesh is willing to make a trade.

Your sin nature is sometimes willing to trade one sin in for another. This is why so many people have become victims of self-righteousness. In exchange for sins like drunkenness, adultery, and stealing, the flesh is willing to trade for pride, superiority, rivalry, condescension, and jealousy. Many very *religious* people have made this trade, like a dark game of go fish. It is not as hard as you might think to trade in unrighteousness for self-righteousness. Both are sins, which is why your sin nature is satisfied with letting you remain self-righteous.

Many think they are pretty righteous when in reality, all they have done is traded in obvious outward sins for inward secret sins. The sad bit is that Jesus seemed much more irritated by self-righteousness, pride, and superiority than drunkenness and adultery. The flesh is not willing to give up sins, which is why you can't force righteousness on your flesh by bodily means.

Have you allowed sins, even small ones, to continue growing in your life? I had years where I did. Many Christians do. Overlooking your sin is one of the most dangerous things you can do. It will stifle your life, change the way you think, harden your heart, and can ultimately lead to death if left unchecked.

It's time that we begin to learn how to change our mindset. In the next section we will explore our first helpful habit; a tool that helps us set our minds on spiritual things.

PART III
PRAYER

31

WEEDING

For a week, Aunt Loola has been visiting each morning. She likes her coffee hot and dark. She comes armed with instructions for you. You've seen little progress so far, but at least you're getting your hands dirty.

"What should we do next?" you ask.

"It's time to do something about these weeds," Loola says.

"Should I just rip them all out?" you ask, cracking your knuckles, readying for action.

"Ripping out every weed isn't necessary for now. The size of the tree's canopy of leaves is usually the size of the roots below the dirt. That's the area we want to focus on first. As the tree grows, we'll expand our weeding," she says.

"Ok, so pull up the weeds that are around the sapling. Got it," you say.

"Yes, but there's more to it than that."

"Oh?" you ask.

"Many of those thorny vines are probably wrapped around the roots. We don't want to simply grab and tear. We'll have to be gentle at first," she says.

“Gentle, no problem.” You step into the garden and reach for your first fistful of weeds.

“Uh, Honey,” Aunt Loola says. “You're going to want gloves. There are some angry thorns in there.”

"Oh yeah," you say before rushing off to the shed. Now gloved, you return and step back into the garden. You kneel and prepare to pull some weeds.

“Now,” Loola says, interrupting you. “What is your weeding schedule going to be?" she asks.

“Schedule?" you say. “I am going to just get it all done now.”

“Oh, you have a time machine, then?”

“I uh— what?”

“You can only take care of the weeds that are here now. More will grow, and you'll have to take care of them when they arise. You can put down mulch which will help keep them from growing, but you'll have to check for weeds on some kind of regular basis," she explains.

“Oh, yeah. I guess that makes sense. How often do you weed your garden?”

“A little every day.”

"Ok, I'll try that then," Now that you have that out of the way, you turn your attention to the garden and prepare.

“Do you know how to weed, Dear?” Loola asks.

“Yeah, of course," you say. *Who doesn't know how to weed,* you don't say.

“Ok, let's see.”

“Are you sure you don't have another speech?"

"I'm sorry, am I disturbing you? I won't say another thing." She draws her fingers across her lips, making a zip tight seal.

You laugh at the playful sarcasm as you lean down low and begin. It feels good to grab, rip, and tear the vines, thorns, and poisonous ivy that has been threatening your fruit tree. You feel like an avenger, taking out sweet retribution on everything wrong in the world. In five minutes, you've shorn the space down to the dirt in a two-foot circle. Your fruit tree can finally soak up the sun.

Pulling off your gloves, you take a seat next to Aunt Loola. You wait for her response.

“So, when are you going to start?" she asks.

“Start what?" You wonder if her eyesight is failing.

“When are you going to start weeding the garden?"

“I just did. Didn't you see me?”

"I saw you give those weeds a haircut," she says.

“I —uh," you stammer. “I pulled up the weeds.”

“Sweetheart. Weeding isn't grabbing, ripping, and tearing," she says. “Weeding is digging. Weeding is removing the whole plant, roots and all.”

“Yeah, I guess I didn't, uh—” you trail off as you look at the garden you just shaved.

“No, you didn't, Honey. You've got to get the right tool. Plus, all you've done is disturb them. Now they are going to feel threatened and grow back twice as hardy.”

"Oh, ok, I'll get a shovel," you say, moving once more toward the shed.

"No, it's too late," Loola says. "Now that you've cropped them stalk and leaf, we can't see where the roots are. We'll have to wait until they grow back. Then we'll weed them right."

32

PRAYER TAKES DIGGING

Weeding is something a gardener must commit to regularly doing. To weed successfully, you have to go deep and get at the roots. Without weeding, there will be little to no fruit. Weeding a certain amount per day isn't the purpose or the goal of gardening, though it's something that needs to be done for gardening success.

This is our analogy for prayer. In your pursuit of abundant life, you need to commit to prayer on some kind of regularity. Your prayer must go deep, which you do by being honest and vulnerable when you talk to the Lord. Without prayer, there is going to be little spiritual fruit. Don't forget, however, that praying a certain amount of your day isn't the ultimate goal of the Christian life.

The ultimate goal is abundant life that comes by transformation. The Spirit transforms you when you set your mind on Spiritual things. This is why prayer is so important. By definition, prayer is placing your mind on things above, in a practiced and deliberate way. In the next few chapters, we'll lay out why and how to pray as we trace the ways in which you can be spiritually transformed by prayer.

33
LAZY

"I'm going out of town for a few days," Loola says over the phone. You flip pancakes on the stove-top skillet. You pinch the phone between your shoulder and your ear.

"Where are you going?"

"I'm going to see my son," she says. "He never comes to town. He's become too important."

"Well, I'm sure he'll be happy to see you."

"I don't know if happy is quite the right word. He says he has something important he wants to talk to me about." She pauses, takes a deep breath, and coughs.

"Are you ok?"

"I'll be fine. It's that fruit tree you should be worried about."

"How many days are you going to be gone? I'll need at least a week to kill it." You reach for the knob on the stove and twist. You stack the pancakes on a plate and head to the table.

"Listen, Honey. You've got to keep weeding. I'm not going to be around to hold your hand to the briar."

"Clever." You slap a log of butter on the cakes and then drown the pile in syrup. You can't stand cold pancakes, so you fill your mouth. Muffled, you say, "It'll be fine. Have a good trip. Don't give your son too hard a time." You say your goodbyes and focus fully on your pancakes.

Doing the dishes, you look out the kitchen window and feel a sense of freedom. You've loved your time with Aunt Loola, but it might be nice to get a break from her constant instructions. There are things you've wanted to do, but knowing Loola will arrive early has kept you focused on gardening. You've thought of little else for months.

With your freedom, you catch up on some chores. You get some bills paid, and some laundry done. You oil that squeaky hinge that squawks when you open the door. By midday, you've met most of your responsibilities. By two you hit the couch and pull out your phone.

"I'll do a little gardening research," you say to the empty room. You go to your favorite video sharing website and search for gardening tips. You watch a few on-topic videos before an adjacent video takes your attention. You click on How To Make The World's Best Pancakes. That leads to bacon infused pancakes, then the world champion pancake flipper. It's on to a video documenting an incident where someone's pancake batter miraculously spilled out into the perfect silhouette of Abraham Lincoln. A local priest declared it a miracle, and now the Lincoln Cake is on display at a church history museum. That video ends with an advertisement for a revolutionary cake batter mixer, which sweeps you away to an online shopping page.

When the sun is down you rise from the warm sweaty indention in the couch, stretching your back and arms. As you pass by the window, you look out at the darkened yard. You had planned to weed, but the time slipped away. "Why weed every day, anyway?" you ask. Though there is no one to hear you, you notice that your tone sounds defensive. "I can let 'em grow, then just get them all at once."

You spend a week's worth of days similarly. You don't make it to your garden a single time. Each day ends with promises to fulfill your Loolaific duties soon. "I'll get around to it before Loola gets back," you tell yourself.

One morning a knock on the front door shakes the house and rattles the windows. You rise, wiping your eyes and stretching away the stiffness. "What time is it?" You glance at the clock. It's early. Really early. It's Loola early. "Oh, no! It's—"

You rush to straighten your hair and throw on clothes. You make it to the door and find Aunt Loola, back from her trip, wearing a particularly satisfied expression on her face.

"I— uh—" you stutter.

"Hello, is the word you're looking for, Honey."

"Of course, hello. Welcome back. Did you—"

"Nope," she says.

"Nope, what?"

"To whatever you were about to ask. The answer is, nope."

"Come in." You scoot out of the way to let her by, but she doesn't budge.

"I'm not here to see you, Honey."

"Oh, the tree. Right." You grip the doorknob as if the house is tilting on its side. "The thing is, I'm really pretty busy today." Loola glances at your bare feet. "Or, I mean I will be. I have to—"

"That's alright," Loola says as she steps off your porch. You expect her to walk toward the street and to her home, but she doesn't. She turns the corner and moves in the direction of your backyard. You gulp hard and follow her.

"Are you sure you don't want to just come back tomorrow?" You chase her around the side of the house and plant yourself in her way. "I mean, you're probably tired from your trip."

"Not a bit. I slept in till five." She smiles. "I'm old, remember."

You follow as she continues to move toward the massive embarrassing mess. As you both approach, you can hardly stand to let your eyes fall on the new tangled overgrowth. The fruit tree stands above it all, but the weeds that surround are half as tall as the burgeoning sapling.

You watch Loola as she steps into the fray of weedy mess and greets the head height fruit tree. "Hey, there," she says. Her warmth surprises you. You wait with a heaviness. You know that at any moment she is going to turn on you and deliver a fiery lecture. Certainly she's going to reprimand you for letting the weeds grow so tall, but she doesn't.

She steps out of the patch of weeds and passes you by. She pats you on the shoulder as she says, "It's good to see you too, Honey." With that, she's on her way.

"But—" you start. "Aren't you disappointed or something? Where's the witty banter, or the cutting criticism?"

"For what?"

"For this," you say as you gesture to the weeds that encircle your feet. "You told me to weed while you were gone. I'm embarrassed that you are seeing the garden like this. I meant to weed it before you got back."

"Oh, no," Loola says as if she's just discovered the problem. Is it possible that she didn't see the weeds? "You meant to weed before I got back? Why?"

"Because, I didn't want you to see it like this. It's a mess."

"So you were going to weed, to please me?" she asks.

"Well— I— uh..."

"That's what you're saying, isn't it? You knew I'd be

displeased, so you were going to weed the garden. Is that what you meant?"

"I— uh—"

"When I left your gardening goal was—?"

"Fruit."

"But now that I'm back, your gardening goal has changed? Your goal is to please me now?" She smiles with a glow that warms you from the inside. "Honey, I'm a terrible reason to work in your garden. You got to get back to your goal."

You look at the ground for a long few moments and then glance to the weedy mess behind you. She rests her arm on your shoulder as she whispers.

"Don't you dare pull any of those weeds to please me. If you decide to uproot 'em, ask yourself with every one of them, why am I pulling this weed? If the answer isn't, fruit, then stop pulling them until it is."

"Thanks, Loola."

"And, Honey. Don't be embarrassed. I've been gone for a week. My garden has just as many weeds as yours. And I know exactly why I'll be pulling them." She points at you, waiting for your response.

"Fruit, abundant fruit."

34

WHY PRAY

I used to meet with a group of men for lunch who were struggling with doubt. One of the repeated questions that came up was, "why are we supposed to pray?" There was a time in my life when I was asking that same question. I asked a pastor friend, "why do we pray?" And he honestly answered, "I don't know." I found his honesty admirable, but his answer frightening.

Have you ever felt that way? Have you ever felt like prayer is a useless waste of time? I've had entire seasons of my life where I hardly prayed at all because of that exact feeling. All of this changed for me a number of years ago, and I'm a die-hard believer in prayer. It has helped me tremendously to understand the purpose of prayer.

So, why do we pray? This is one way that Paul answered that question in a letter to his friends in Philippi, "pray and ask God for everything you need, always giving thanks for what you have; and the peace of God, which surpasses all understanding, will guard your hearts and minds through Christ Jesus.[1]

What you need is a never-ending focus and reliance on the Spirit's power, which is able to transform you. You need a mindset that stays focused on God and godly things. Paul says that when you pray, God's peace, which is beyond understanding, will guard your mind. Prayer is armor for your mindset. His peace wraps around your frazzled and worrisome mind when you pray so that you can remain focused on the Spirit. Prayer quiets the world full of distractions so that you can allow your mind to do what it is supposed to do, focus on God.

Prayer is designed to focus your mindset on spiritual things. Each time you pray, you hand your worries over to God so that you can maintain your focus. All of this is to accomplish the ultimate goal, which to have an abundant and fruitful life. When you maintain a spiritual mindset, God's power is released into your life. Prayer is the best way to keep that spiritual mindset alive.

Some might ask, "how much should I pray?" I would return that question with another question. "How much abundant life do you want?" Pray in proportion to the amount of spiritual fruit you wish to have. Do you want more joy? Ask God for it. Do you want more peace? Ask the Lord. Do you want more love? It's His will for you to have that, so ask. In fact, each time you sense your mind swerving off of its target, pray. This practice will get the mind back where it's supposed to be.

In answering, "how much should I pray?" It would be easy to give you a time requirement to fulfil, but I think that's the wrong approach. The flesh wants a box to check, a to-do list, a quota to fill. The Spirit seeks your heart. It's a different approach altogether. Remember, the ultimate goal is not to spend a certain amount of time in prayer. The ultimate goal of your time remaining on earth is to experience abundant life. The danger of turning your prayer time into a mechanical ritual is that it can become meaningless repetition, said without sincerity. That defeats the purpose.

Prayer is a tool that will help you achieve abundant life when you do it sincerely. Jesus even offers a model for prayer that we can follow. (more on that in the next few chapters) Setting a quota for prayer time can easily shove you into being a *lifestyle legalist.* Let's avoid that. A great rule of thumb is to pray as often as you need, to focus your mind on Spiritual things. Let the need for maintaining a Spiritual mindset guide how much you pray.

Let me illustrate this concept. I used to have a very used car which was badly out of alignment. It was the kind of car you couldn't nod off in even for a second because it would automatically steer itself off the road. That terrible steering would pull me toward the ditch, where a collision would mean my untimely death. Your flesh wants to pull your mind into the ditch, where death waits. Prayer is your first weapon against the swerve. In the same way that I would correct the steering each time it pulled to the right or the left, we must correct our swerving minds with prayer. This is why Paul said, *pray constantly.*[2]

You might feel intimidated by prayer. It might be one of the divine mysteries that you've never cracked. You may even feel as if your prayers bounce off the ceiling, or maybe they're not even getting that far. Prayer can be a daunting task, but it really doesn't have to be. Paul offers hope.

Paul explains one of the methods for accomplishing it when he says, *We don't know how to pray as we should, but the Spirit himself speaks to God for us. He begs God for us, speaking to him with groans too deep for words. God already knows our deepest thoughts. And he understands what the Spirit is saying because the Spirit speaks for his people in the way that agrees with what God wants.*[3] This is great news. You don't have to be a perfect prayer expert. When you pray to God, the Spirit speaks on your behalf. When you offer up your sincere requests, the Spirit fills in the gaps.

Growing up, I had a brother who was fairly quiet. I often found myself speaking on his behalf. I would answer questions for him, even when someone addressed him directly. He seemed pleased enough to have someone close to him be his mouthpiece. Now, I was an amateur, but the Spirit is an expert. The Spirit takes your broken and imperfect prayers and explains what you need to God, and makes requests on your behalf. The Spirit knows God's will, so the requests the Spirit makes on your behalf are both in your best interests but also in alignment with God's will. Thank you, Holy Spirit!

There's more good news. Jesus said, *Pray to your Father… and he will reward you.*[4] If you pray in the way that Jesus teaches, there will be a reward. God rewards us both in this life and the life to come. Our focus, for now, is on the reward we receive in this life for praying to Him. What is the reward for prayer? Simply stated, it's a more Abundant life!

Prayer, by its very nature, is an action you can perform that focuses your mind on that which is Spiritual. If you are sincerely praying, not just mindlessly reciting meaningless words, it forces your mind to focus on God and godly concepts. When you do this, the Spirit is active. He is busy when you pray, acting as an advocate and translator. That spiritual activity works on your mindset, which releases the Spirit's power of transformation into your life. It even changes the way you will act. This is why prayer is so incredibly important.

How do I pray? You may ask. If you asked a hundred

different people how to pray, you would get a hundred different answers. Luckily, Jesus' gave a beginner's guide to prayer. In the next section, we'll take a look at how Jesus taught us to pray.

35

A GARDEN TRANSFORMED

"That's how it's done," Loola says from her garden chair. She's watching you remove weeds with your trusty hand shovel. The place that has been wild for so long is beginning to look respectable. For weeks now, you've removed weeds with careful yet thorough digging. "What a difference weeding makes!"

"Yeah. It's starting to look like I know what I'm doing," you say as you stand and step next to Loola's honorary garden side seat. You grab your water bottle as she reaches out with her coffee cup to clink it against yours. When you reach out, she places her palm on the back of your hand.

"Honey, I'm proud of you," she says, looking up. Her face is rimmed in morning sun.

"Thanks, Aunt Loola."

"The beauty of transformation," she says as she looks back toward the garden. You nod, but you can't take your eyes off the little fruit tree that stands proudly at the center of a weed-free patch of soil.

"Hey, look!" You point. Nearly leaping, you spring toward the little tree and kneel before it. Your eyes grow to the size of apricots as you investigate one of the sprigs that shoots from the tiny trunk. "It's a bud!" You are virtually shouting now. "It's growing fruit." You look back to Aunt Loola, who hasn't risen from her seat, though a wide smile is stretched across her face.

"The transformation has begun," she says.

"Now I can just sit back and let the fruit roll in, right?" you say, with an ironic smile.

"Don't get cocky."

"Come on," you say. "It's finally working; I could take at least a little weeding vacation, couldn't I?"

"One-half ounce of success, and you're ready to step off the scale."

"That's not a saying," you argue.

"Well, I said it, didn't I?" she says. She points at the slim little branch with its burgeoning sprout. "Can you eat that fruit?"

"Well, I could but—" you begin to say, but Loola cuts you off.

"No, no, no. Does that fruit qualify as abundant?" she rephrases.

"No," you say with a laugh. By now, you have gotten good at sensing when one of Aunt Loola's lectures is about to begin. Now is one of those times.

"If that tree doesn't transform, you'll never taste a single mouthful of fruit. This is the beginning of the metamorphosis, but it's far from the end. Every weed you pull allows that tree to transform into what it needs to be to accomplish its grand gardening goal."

"Yeah. I know," you say. "I just like to see you get all steamed up and speechful."

"You're taunting an old woman, you know? There's probably a law against that," she says. "What's the goal?"

"Fruit, abundant fruit."

"And what does that tree need to do to achieve it?" she asks.

"Transform!"

"And how can you help it transform?"

"Keep weeding like the Prison guards' chain gang gardaner."

"That's right," she says as she slaps the arm of her garden chair. "But there's more to it than that."

"So, what do I need to do?" you ask.

"It's good to remove weeds that have already come up, but we also need to prevent new weeds from taking root."

"And how do we do that?"

"It's a war of attrition. We have to lay siege to the soil," she says.

"I don't have a catapult."

"Mulch will do it," she explains.

"Oh, ok. I don't have any mulch, either" you say, but then add, "I could go get some from the store when I go—"

"Nah, no need," she says. "You've got mulch right here." She points to the ground.

"Uh— I don't get it."

"What does mulch do?" she asks.

"Well, it—"

"It' lays siege to the soil, of course," she picks up a handful of leaves from the ground. "It blocks the sun from hitting the soil so that no new weeds can grow."

"So, I can just put a layer of leaves on the soil, and then I don't have to weed anymore?"

"I'm reluctant to admit that it actually *will* make your job a little easier?" she says. "But there will still be some weeds that get through. There's no release from this chain gang, Honey."

36

BEGINNER'S GUIDE TO PRAYER

Many people feel intimidated by prayer. They aren't sure how to start. In this section, I'd like to use Jesus' teaching on prayer as a beginner's guide. He tells us how to do it and even makes it easy.

I bet you know the Lord's Prayer. It starts off, "Our Father, who art in Heaven. Hallowed be thy name..." You know it, right? Many people do. I have it memorized quite by accident. Strangely, the version I accidentally memorized is in the King James Version, but I hardly have ever used King James. This means that somewhere in my childhood, I learned the Lord's Prayer, not from my church or personal prayer time, but from some other source. I'm pretty sure it came by hearing it before sporting events, reinforced by being quoted in moves and TV shows, back when prayer could still be heard in popular entertainment.

Let's take a quick look at how Jesus says we should use his prayer template. First, He says that His prayer model is to be used in private.[1] Second, His example prayer isn't to be repeated verbatim over and over again.[2] We're supposed to use

His prayer's ideas, but not the exact words. Third, the praying person is to pray this way on a daily basis.[3] We are supposed to learn His model prayer and then use it as a template for our own private, daily prayer time.

Certainly, an entire book could be written on how to pray according to Jesus' model, but I'd like to keep this simple; so simple, in fact, that you can pray according to Jesus' model right now. If you're comfortable with it, you might try based on the breakdown below.

PRAYER ACCORDING TO JESUS

"OUR FATHER IN HEAVEN..."

Pray to God, as your father, remembering the assurance you have as His child.

"Hallowed be Your name...."

Praise the Lord with some personal expressions of worship.

"Your kingdom come...."

Pray for the Lord's return and the establishment of his Heavenly Kingdom to come.

"Your will be done, On earth as it is in heaven...."

Pray about some ways the Lord's will could be done and how you can take part in bringing that about.

. . .

"GIVE us this day our daily bread...."

Pray that the Lord would provide for the needs you have today and in the near future.

"AND FORGIVE US OUR SINS...."

Confess any known sins and ask the Lord for forgiveness.

"AS WE FORGIVE those who have sinned against us...."

Ask the Lord for the strength to forgive those who have wronged you, and commit to doing so.

"AND DO NOT LEAD us into temptation...."

Pray that the Lord would help you avoid potential temptations, known and unknown.

"BUT DELIVER US FROM EVIL...."

Ask the Lord to help you escape without sinning from any temptation you may fall into today.

"FOR YOURS IS the kingdom and the power and the glory forever."

Acknowledge that God has the power to accomplish all you've asked Him for, and thank Him for what he will do.

"AMEN."

Conclude by saying Amen.

. . .

THIS METHOD of prayer has been a life-changer for me. There are days when I pray through this model in a minute or two. There are days when I'm in a deeper spiritual need, and I will spend more time on this. I generally pray through this model in the morning. Then throughout the day, I may say little prayers about specific things. I try to at least pray through the Lord's template once a day, but there are certainly days that I miss doing it.

When I skip or more often realize that my busyness has kept me from praying, I often recognize a difference in the amount of patience, joy, peace, and love I feel during the day. There is no quota to fill with this. Instead, we should view Jesus' template as one of the greatest tools we have in keeping our minds focused on Him.

I used to feel like prayer was a mystery. There are still days when it's hard or laborious, but at least I know what I'm supposed to do. If I don't do it, it's not because I'm confused. It's just because I'm unfocused. That's why I love praying according to Jesus' template because it takes the guesswork out of my entire prayer life. Jesus told me to pray in this manner, so I do it. On top of that, I know that even if I do it wrong, the Spirit intervenes on my behalf, filling in the gaps that I miss.[4]

I think the simplicity is beautiful. It might just be why Jesus said, *the load I give you to carry is light.*[5] He made it easy. He made it simple. Not only did He tell us how to pray, but He placed His Spirit inside of us to help us every step of the way.

What's the result of an active prayer practice? Mindset shift, which leads to transformation, which leads to abundant life. Remember, the ultimate goal is not to pray a certain amount every day. The ultimate goal is to have a life filled with the fruits of the Spirit. When you pray to the Lord, it sets your mindset in the right place. The result is *love, joy, peace, patience, kindness, goodness, faithfulness, gentleness, and self-control.*[6]

Pray as you eagerly await these Spiritual fruits to grow in your life.

37

PRUNING

You're standing at your kitchen sink staring out at the lawn. What a splendid scene. The sun is smiling down; the grass is still shrouded with dew; the tool shed door is wide and tools are flying out. Wait, what? You set your coffee cup down next to the sink and start toward the exit.

Once you're in the rear, there is no doubt about it. Someone or something is in your tool shed. A clatter confirms it. A spare glove comes flying out of the darkness. Tools are strewn across the ground. You pick up a shovel and hold it like a weapon as you approach.

"Ahh, there you are," Aunt Loola's voice sings out from within the gloom. She strides into the light carrying a pair of hand fitted pruning shears. "I was looking for you."

"Why were you looking for me in the shed?" you inquire as you abandon the shovel and surrender your defensive position.

"No, not you, Honey," she smirks. "I know right where

you were; your bed." She holds up the pruning shears. "I was looking for these."

"Oh, I didn't know I had those," you say. You gather the few tools that have been spread around the entrance and drag them through the barn door. "Wow."

"You like it?" Loola says. "It was a mess, so I organized it." You stare astonished at the newly arranged shed. There is a place for everything. Loola grabs the tools from your hands. "Those are the last of them." She puts the shovel and its comrades in their new place.

"Thank you," you say. "It looks great."

"Yes, yes. There's no time for all that. This tree ain't going to prune itself."

"We're going to prune the fruit tree?"

"That's right."

"But, it's looking so healthy." You follow Loola to the budding and leafy sapling. You don't want to sound defensive, but you can hardly help but protest. "Seems like we should just let it grow. I mean, won't we hurt it if we prune it now?"

"We'll hurt it if we don't."

"But, it just seems like—"

"Listen, Honey," Loola interrupts. "What's the goal?"

"Fruit, but—"

"No. It's not 'fruit but.'"

"Just fruit, I mean."

"Oh. I see. If your goal is just fruit, there's no need to prune. If you just want fruit; miniature, minuscule, microscopic fruit, then don't prune," she pauses. "Is that what you want." You shake your head. "Let's start over. What is your goal? And if you say, 'just fruit' again, I'm going to trim your fingers with these pruning shears." She snaps them aggressively in the air between the two of you.

"Fruit, abundant fruit." Your tone isn't passionate, but you can't help but grin a little.

"Ahh, if it's abundant fruit you want, then we need to prune." She steps around the tree and scans it closely. Her feet crunch in the layer of natural mulch you've laid. You can't resist interrogating her.

"So, why do we prune?"

"Same reason you manage your budget. You've only got so much money, and you have to decide how to spend what you've got."

"So, we're teaching the tree 'financial literacy?'"

"Yes," she says as she reaches for a cluster of leafy branches. "Well, yes and no. We're teaching the tree, yes. Nickel and dime, no." She drops the branch and handles another. "Every cut communicates with the tree. Cutting is communicating."

"Communicating?"

"Yeah. Just like a second ago. I threatened to trim your fingers. I think I was communicating pretty effectively. Don't you?" You close your hands into fists, just to be safe.

"So what are we communicating?"

"The tree is not intelligent enough to know where it should spend its energy. We're looking to trim back about a third of the branches. Take away anything that the tree is focusing energy on which won't result in fruit."

"So, it's a bit of an overspender. We're helping it balance its energy budget."

"Quite right," Loola says. "Ok, you better get to it. We're burning daylight." She gestures for you to take the pruning shears. You grab them and turn toward the tree. "Do you have any alcohol?"

"Is this one of those jobs where it's better to be drunk?"

"No, not that kind of alcohol. Rubbing alcohol. It's good

to sterilize your shears so you don't carry disease from one plant to another."

"These have never been used," you say, holding up the shears. "In fact, I forgot I had them, until you cleaned up the shop. Thanks, by the way—"

"Oh, Alright. You're welcome. Now don't mention it." She waves her hand.

"So where do I cut?"

"You're looking for the three Ds- dead, dying, and diseased." You survey the tree and spot a cluster of brown leaves. You point at it and glance at Loola for approval. She nods. You trim. Once you do, she steps closer.

"Now move back three or four leafy nodes from where you just cut and trim the stalk off at a forty five degree angle." She points to indicate the place she means. "That makes sure no more of that dead wood remains." You do it and turn your attention to the other branches.

"I guess that's it," you say.

"Who taught you math?"

"Uh—"

"I said we need to trim back a third of the tree."

"Ok, so how do we pick what to trim now?"

"CCA," she says. "Clusters, crossings, and acutes. Look at the ends of the branches. See how they tend to cluster up with lots of leafy jumbles. Ain't no fruit go'n come from that. Lop it off."

You find six different spots to chop the tips off of branches. The tree looks more manageable now. You try to repeat the acronym. "Clusters, then was it crossings?"

"Yeah, any place two branches cross at odd angles." You find another handful of those and trim them out.

"What was the last one?"

"Acutes."

"Ok, I don't know what that is."

"This is my favorite part," she says. "We want a goblet shape. You know what a goblet is, right?"

"Like an old school drinking glass?"

"Yeah. So, acutes means you trim any branch that is jutting out at an acute angle. If the branches' angles are too sharp, they won't be able to bear the weight of the fruit. When you're done the whole tree ought to look like a wine glass."

You find another group of branches to trim and drop them to the ground. You step back from the tree. "I guess that's about a third."

"Nice," she says. "Now why did we do this?" Apparently, it's quiz time.

"To help the tree focus its energy on making fruit."

"Making just fruit?" Loola asks.

"No," you sing it out now. "Big, fat, juicy, abundant fruit."

"I can taste it already," she says and then turns back toward the shed. "Ok, come on. It's going to rain." You look at the sky. There isn't a cloud in sight.

38
TRANSFORMED BY CONFESSION

Likely, no one likes confessing their sins. It's for good reason that pruning is our analogy for confession. This can be an uncomfortable activity, but just like pruning a fruit tree, it's absolutely vital. It helps us focus our spiritual energy on the things that need to be trimmed out of our lives. So how exactly does confession work?

As you pray through the Lord's prayer, you will notice that Jesus has instructed that we seek forgiveness for our sins regularly. You can see this in the line of the Lord's Prayer template when he teaches us to say something like, *and forgive us our sins.*[1]

The fact that Jesus tells us to seek forgiveness on a daily basis might surprise some people. *Don't we already have forgiveness?* A believer might ask. Absolutely. You have the kind of forgiveness that allows you to have and keep eternal life. However, if you want abundant life, you need to work on your relationship with the Lord.

Paul touched on this idea in his letter to his friends in Rome when he said, *the sinful nature is always hostile to God. It never did obey God's laws, and it never will. That's why those who are still under the control of their sinful nature can never please God.*[2] When you sin, it's taken as hostility toward God. It displeases Him. What a relief that we've been made eternally right with God by Jesus' death. However, it is still displeasing to Him when we sin.

It displeases me when my daughter hits her brother. It doesn't endanger her place in the family, but it means that I have to respond. In fact, as I was writing this chapter, I could see her do that exact thing through my office window. At this point, she has wronged her brother and upset the balance of the house, which I'm charged to maintain. If she denies it, or worse yet, says her brother deserved the blow, then my displeasure grows. I'm forced not to move on from the situation until she makes it right. I insist upon it. However, if she confesses what she's done and seeks forgiveness that's good enough for me. I can head back to my office and not think about it again.

In a sense, this is what we are expected to do daily. If we want to experience abundant life, we must be confessing our sins on the regular. Now, remember, the ultimate goal is not to be a person who is constantly harping on our own failures. The purpose is to remove anything that blocks us from having abundant life. The first step in this process is to confess our known sin.

In his letter to some very mature believers, the Apostle John explained the mechanics of confession when he said, *But if we confess our sins to him, he is faithful and just to forgive us our sins and to cleanse us from all wickedness.*[3] John's letter is written primarily to tell Christians how to gain and maintain fellowship with each other and with God. In that pursuit, he shows the importance of confession. This daily confession has nothing to do with whether or not you will get into heaven.

You settled that question the moment you believed in Jesus for salvation. This confession has everything to do with the quality of your relationship with God, other believers, and thus the quality of your life.

When you confess the sins you are aware of, God cleanses you of *all unrighteousness.* This means you don't have to be a perfect confessor. You don't have to keep an obsessive logbook, charting every infraction to the Nth degree. Instead, confess the sins you are aware of, ask God for forgiveness, and trust that he's forgiven them. He said he would, so believe it.

I know for years, especially back in the days when I was looking at porn. I would sometimes confess, but it seemed a bit ridiculous. I would admit in prayer that I had sinned again, but I was also convinced that I would be doing the same sin the following night. I got to where I didn't confess at all because I misunderstood what confession was.

Somewhere along the way, someone had told me that confession involves a promise to quit. They had clearly mixed up the meaning since confession is simply admitting the truth. I had begun to think, with my porn habit, that if I "confessed" but then fell into the sin again, then my confession was faulty. If you've found yourself in that kind of mentality, take a step back because that's not what is being said here.

Confession is simply admitting the failure to God and asking him for forgiveness. Changing the habit is a separate process that we'll talk about in a later chapter. Confession is simpler than many make it. In your prayer time, simply think through your recent memory and consider anything that might be sin. I sometimes ask God to reveal to me my recent sins. Any that I identify, I confess, ask forgiveness for, and thank God for his mercy.

This is part of what John calls *...living in the light,*[4] and you can see why. When we confess, we are simply bringing our sins into the light. It forces us to take a well-lit look at how we are doing and the areas we need God's help with.

John explains that *If we claim to have fellowship with him and yet walk in the darkness, we lie ... If we claim to be without sin, we deceive ourselves and the truth is not in us.*[5] There are lots of saved people who are not living in fellowship with God because they don't confess their sins. If you want to maintain a close friendship with the Lord, you need to live in the light, which includes regular confession.

This is one of the reasons I love the Lord's Prayer template. If you follow it, you get confession as a package deal. There is another thing that you get in this packaged deal, which we will talk about in the next chapter.

39
STORM

The wind whistles outside your bedroom window and the roof creaks with the howling blast. You sit up in bed and peer toward the clock. It's dark, as is the entire house. Outside, a fierce crack punctuates the screaming bluster. You sneak to the window, as if the storm might discover you're out of bed.

Rain pours down in blinding sheets. The street is dark. The aggression rages on as you move back to your bed and shelter beneath the covers. You close your eyes but do not dream until hours later.

The next morning you wake tired. Your clock flashes as if to blink away the memory of that midnight tumult. You climb out of bed and put on enough clothes to go outside.

Leaves and branches are strewn about the yard, but thankfully there isn't any obvious damage to the house. You turn toward your fruit tree, hoping all is well. You gasp as you approach. It feels like a funeral. In the wake of the grave storm, there stands a mangled mess. Broken branches dangle from the pitiful tree. You don't touch it.

Instinctively, you rush toward the house where your phone waits. Your feet carry quick on the heels of the tragedy. Your mind races as your body moves with lightning instinct through the house.

"Loola," you hear your own words as if from a distance. "It's the tree. It broke in the storm." You're surprised at the urgency in your voice. It isn't until this moment you realize all the tree means to you.

"I'll be right over."

"No!" you are forceful. "I'll come get you." Her enthusiasm is admirable, but her walking speed leaves something to be desired. You're in the car in a flash, and in front of her house in mere moments. She comes out carrying a small bag. You're in too much of a hurry to ask about the contents. Once to your house, in a blur, you rush her to the carnage.

"Yep. That's a broken tree, alright."

"Is there anything we can do?"

"Of course." She moves around the tree cautiously. She handles the broken branches with the most delicate care. "It's not as bad as it looks."

"It's not?" You move close, holding your breath as if a gasp could kill the tree. She points as she talks.

"All branches, but one still have some of their cambium and phloem layers connected. That means we can repair 'em." You let out the breath you've been holding.

She hands you her small bag and points toward the zipper. You open it and hold it out. She reaches for a roll of something. "Grafting tape," she says. "Here, I'll show you how."

She gently takes one of the broken branches and straightens it. She squeezes the broken place between her fingers. "Now wrap the break. Do it tight. Cover the entire broken place."

You send the grafting tape around in methodical circles,

pulling tension with every pass. "Good," she says in a whisper. You both let go of the branch. "Now, trim off the fruit buds from this branch so that they don't weigh it down." You do as she instructs. When you're done, you move on to the next branch. The process is comfortable by the time you get to the third branch.

"What about this one?" You ask, picking up a branch the storm has completely severed.

"You choose," she says with a smile. "We could trim the broken place back and leave it as is, or we could try to graft that branch back on."

"Graft? Do you mean we could reattach it?"

"It might take, it might not, but it's worth learning the technique."

"Ok, let's do that." She reaches into the bag you're holding and pulls a knife from the interior. Instead of doing the work, she hands you the sheathed blade. She picks up the broken branch and offers it into your hands.

"Cut the broken part away at a sharp angle," she says as she points. You take the knife and make a diagonal cut. It's pretty shabby, so you try again. You get it right on the third try. She uses her fingernail to point at the exposed wood around the edge of the sliced branch.

"That's the cambium layer. You've got to make sure that comes in contact with the cambium of the branch we're grafting onto. We're going to use a whip and tongue technique."

"Tongue and whip?" you ask, feeling an urge to make a corny joke. Loola must sense your distraction.

"Focus," she says. "Now make a backward cut about halfway up the diagonal slice." She marks the spot with her fingernail and shows you how to hold the knife. Once you've made the cut, you glance at her for approval. She nods and points to the spot where the branch broke off the tree. "Now, we do the same there."

You work to imitate the same cuts on the tree. As you slice, she talks. "You know, pretty much no one plants a fruit tree from seed anymore."

"How do they do it?" You hold up the two branches to see if your cuts line up.

"They use the rootstock from one tree and then graft on the species of branches that will grow the fruit they want. You can have a dozen different fruits on one tree. If you're going to be growing fruit, learning to graft is a must."

"How's that?" You hold up your work. She nods.

"Now, they should slide together." You push the whip and tongue graft into its mate. It drives in with a satisfying tightness. "Ok, wrap it with the tape." You encircle the graft with a few dozen passes and step back from the tree. It looks like a soldier who's just come from the medic's tent, but it's in one piece again.

Loola pats you on the shoulder and says, "You sure are grafty."

"And you didn't even have to whip or tongue."

40

REQUEST TRANSFORMATION

Life is packed with its little (and sometimes big) emergencies. Just like a sapling in a storm, sometimes we have to figure out how to graft our lives back together, or better yet avoid breaking down in the first place. How do we handle life's emergencies?

Jesus said we ought to daily pray, *do not lead us into temptation, But deliver us from evil.*[1] If you pray according to the Lord's prayer, you will daily be asking for help to overcome your sin. As we pray this, God will transform us according to our request and His will.

This is in line with what Paul says when he explains we need to, *put to death the deeds of the flesh.*[2] Whether you realize it or not, it's sin that is keeping you from abundant life. If you had no sin, your life would be abundant by default. However, since you are still living in the sinful flesh, your life is less abundant than it could be.

There are scheduled prayers, and there are emergency prayers. The Lord's Prayer template is a great model for scheduled daily private prayer. However, sometimes we need to make an emergency call on the red telephone. On a daily basis, when I fall into temptation to sin, I offer up emergency prayers for help to escape without committing the sin.

These emergency prayers don't follow the entirety of the Lord's Prayer template. They borrow just a line here and there. They are snippets, custom fit for the situation at hand. Emergency prayers, for me, are all about escaping temptation and avoiding sin by re-setting my mind on things above. These little one-liners are designed to realign my mind in a hurry. An example of a common emergency prayer for me is, "Lord, take that thought out of my mind." It's all about my mindset.

Sometimes I call this *bombing the tracks.* Imagine an enemy train rolling down the railroad. You have to call in an airstrike before the train reaches the tunnel. As soon as you call, the dive bombers appear and drop a thousand mega tons of explosives on the railroad tracks and obliterate the train's path forward. The train derails, and the day is saved.

In this little analogy, the enemy locomotive is your train of thought. You can sense when your thought train is rolling in the wrong direction, toward the dark tunnel of sin. This very moment is when you need to make an emergency call. Bring in the big guns. Ring the red telephone in Heaven. You need to ask God to help you remove that thought process. You need him to bomb the tracks that train of thought is riding on. Without fail, when I wind up sinning is when I don't call in the airstrike. The train of thought reaches its destination, and I end up acting on the thoughts. We have to ask God to deliver us from our own mindset in the very moment of temptation.

The way to focus your mental power on God is to constantly call out to Him for deliverance when your mind wanders to those dark places. You ought to do this in a scheduled way when you pray through the Lord's prayer. However, you should also use the emergency prayer concept when you fall into temptation. Call out to the Lord in the very moment you are being tempted, and he'll provide a way out.

This is how you will bring your rotting deeds into the light and murder them in the blazing radiation power of the Spirit that God has placed inside of you. It's the same Spirit that brought Jesus back from the dead.[3] If He can bring life to a dead body, then He can put to death the sin in your flesh. Your greatest tool in overcoming your sin isn't your willpower, determination, or gut-level resolve. It's your open request line that rings the situation-room of Heaven. The Spirit is ready to go to war against your flesh, at your request. What you need to do is ask.

Maybe it's kind of like one of those low-budget action movies from the 90s. You've been plagued by a dark monster that lurks in the shadowy landscape of your flesh. You've tried everything you know. Now, you have to hire a gunslinger with a monster-killing talent. You need a hitman to take down the beast. God's Spirit is *the* monster killer. That Spirit that lives within you is ready to rain down repeated death blows upon your sin. The best part is, He works for free. Simply call out to God in the moments when that sin monster is dogging you, and he will step to the front and unload both smoking barrels with white-hot blasts of fiery vengeance.

Do you know what would make a terrible movie? Imagine calling the monster hunter to town and then having him ride the bench; having access to the gunslinger but telling him to sit this one out. The monster pulverizes you, while the expert is forced to stand by and watch. "Do you want me to take care of that?" the gunslinger asks. "It kind of looks like he's got you down." The monster continues to pound you while you respond listlessly to the hired gun, "Nope, I've got 'em right where I want him." The words barely escape your lips as the sin beast crushes you to the floor and snarls inches from your face.

That's what you do every time you DON'T ask for God's help in the moment of temptation. He's ready to lead you out without a scratch.[4] He's ready to unload his double-barrel boom-stick on the evil beast that lurks in your bones, but you decline the help, thinking you can handle the growling monster in your own effort.

I remember the first time I recognized that it was possible to win against temptation. It was when I was in college. I was plagued by lust. I entertained many sinful thoughts. I knew that the thoughts running through my head were wrong. I was committing adultery in my heart, as Jesus put it.[5] One of my favorite bands has a lyric that says, "There's no difference in the things that happen in my head and happen in my bed."[6] That was the kind of sinful defeat I was experiencing on a regular basis, and I was sick of it.

I was lying on my bed one night. My mind was moving toward that familiar sin. I was creeping in the direction of the old lust habit. I felt helpless and incapable of stopping the images that began to rush in. At that very moment, I called out to God. "Help me!" I said aloud. "I don't want this sin. Take this garbage away from my mind."

To my amazement, something actually happened. My mind cleared, and I got relief from the monster that lives inside. I could hardly believe it actually worked. "Thank you," I said to the Lord, very surprised. I was astonished that it actually made a difference. I now realize that what happened at that moment was exactly what Paul talks about in his letter to his friends in Rome.

I prayed to God. I cried out to Him. I put my mind on Him by requesting His help. In that pivotal moment, the all-powerful Spirit of God stepped to the front, shoved me behind, and blocked the fiery attack of the enemy. I was astounded that it worked, but what is more astounding is how often I have NOT taken advantage of the power that lives inside.

Over and over, after that point, I let the waves of lust wash over me, often until my flesh would act on what was in my mind. How sad it is that I've so often resisted putting my mind in the right place by calling out for God's help.

This is how you beat sin. You pray for God's help at the moment you are being tempted and you keep praying until the monster killer does His work.

Notice how Paul puts it, *If by the Spirit you put to death the deeds of the flesh, you will live.*[7] Notice that incredibly important phrase, *by the Spirit.* If you decide you want to go it alone, relying on your own grit and determination, you can expect to fail. If you're willing to request help from the power that God placed inside you, then He will transform you, and you will experience abundant life.

I think this is why Paul later says, *Do not be conformed to this world but be transformed by the renewing of your mind.*[8] Where does the request for Spiritual help come from? It comes from your mind. You ask God, often silently, for help, and He supplies. You set your mind on God, calling to Him for help, and it will be the Spirit that transforms you. Just like a sprig that transforms into a fruit-laden tree, God's Spirit will transform you into a person who experiences abundant life.

Paul once said to his young friend, *Timothy, flee from youthful passions, and pursue righteousness, faith, love, and peace, along with those who call on the Lord from a pure heart.*[9] Notice what he's saying. If you want God to transform you into a person who is righteous, filled with love, peace, and faith, then you need to call on the Lord for help. Transformation comes by request. You can't accomplish abundant life by trying to get your flesh to behave. It comes by calling upon God for help. You don't force transformation directly; you ask God for the change and he supplies.

It's simple but not necessarily easy. It isn't easy to call for help from God in the moment of your temptation. Your flesh will be screaming at you to stay silent. Your flesh wants the pleasures promised. However, if you call out to God for help while you're being tempted, it changes everything. The times that I have asked for help, especially at the precise moment I need it, the help comes.

This is another reason why I love the Lord's Prayer template. If you follow it daily, you will be asking the Lord for deliverance from sin and for help in avoiding temptation daily. It's another one of those package deals. When you follow the prayer Jesus gave us, you're daily asking for transformation. You add a turbo boost when you send up an emergency prayer, a snippet like, "Lord, lead me out of *this* temptation, and deliver me from *this* evil!" He's happy to answer that prayer! He promises to provide a way out.

PART IV
SCRIPTURE

41
THE ALMANAC

A few weeks of weeding has made a stupendous change in the look of your one-tree orchard. The fruit tree is finally beginning to grow. You've diligently dug up any weeds that are hardy enough to make it through the layer of mulch. Things are beginning to look respectable in your fledgling fruit garden. Aunt Loola still visits, but often just to chat. One fine morning her bright voice breaks the silence.

"Ah, a gardener's work is never done," she says. You rise to see her approaching through the yard, cane in hand. She moves slower than usual. She finds the way to her seat, where you made sure to set out her dark coffee before she arrived.

"A gardener's work is never done because a gardener's mentor never gets tired of seeing her student pulling weeds," you say with a laugh. You pause from your work and take up your place next to aunt Loola. You notice a package she has neatly placed on her lap.

"How are you today?" you ask.

"Old," she says. "At least that's what my kids say."

"What?" you protest. "You are young enough to walk over here every morning."

"Well, actually, I was driven here today," she says.

"By whom?"

"My son. He's waiting in the car, and I raised him to be very impatient, apparently," she says. You're surprised. Her son lives hours away.

"Is everything ok, Aunt Loola?" you ask.

"Yes, but—" she breaks. "This will be the last time I get to come see you." You detect the faintest trace of wetness around her eyes.

"I'll come to your house for our visits; I don't mind," you say.

"That would be a long commute," she grins, but the expression doesn't quite touch her eyes. "My Son is kidnapping me. He insists that I move in with him. He thinks I'm too old to take care of myself anymore. And you know, he's probably right. I just keep making my coffee darker, but it doesn't seem to speed me up any."

"No," you argue. "I could have a talk with him."

"No, he's a big city lawyer," she counters. "It's impossible to change his mind."

"Well, I—" you start to say but run short on words. You reach out and hug Aunt Loola, not knowing what else to do.

"It's ok; he needs some serious help with his garden. He's let it go to weeds," she says.

"Probably makes his coffee too weak, too," you add.

"It's just frothy milk with a gun shot blast of espresso." She smiles. "His momma will straighten him out."

"I can't thank you enough for everything you've taught me and for your friendship," you say.

"Well, I have a little something for you," she says as she

reaches for the package in her lap. “I made my son pay for it, so I guess technically it’s from him.”

"Well, tell him, 'thank you,'" you say as you take the package from her outstretched hands. It has a satisfying weight. You open it eagerly to find a book. "Oh, this is great."

"It's a Gardener's Almanac," Loola says. "During my soon coming imprisonment, you'll need someone to tell you what to do. This book is written by experts and has everything you need to know on how to bring this little orchard to harvest."

As Aunt Loola rises, you hug her once more and offer your arm to lean on as she begins to move slowly toward her son's car. It's hard to say goodbye, but you do reluctantly. It feels like there is a hole in your heart as you watch aunt Loola drive away. You clutch the book she gave you, as the reminder of what she means to you.

42

YOUR OWN BIBLE

For a gardening beginner, gardening books are a valuable resource. None, it seems, has spanned the test of time like the Farmer's Almanac. In the standard format, you can find the information you need to become a successful planter, grower, and harvester.

In the story, the Gardener's Almanac is our allegory for Scripture. It seems that in the early church, it was thought that Jesus would return to the earth before that first generation had passed away. In fact, we see evidence of this in the Gospel of John. Toward the end of his Gospel, John explains a misunderstanding that had cropped up in the church. In a conversation between John, Jesus, and Peter, Jesus had said to Peter, *Maybe I want him [John] to live until I come… So a story spread among the followers of Jesus. They were saying that this follower [John] would not die. But Jesus did not say he would not die. He only said, "Maybe I want him to live until I come.*[1]

Because of this misunderstanding and their intense eagerness to see Jesus return, the early church believed that Jesus would come back before John died. It didn't happen that way. Instead, we are still waiting eagerly for Jesus's return.

The reason I bring it up is related to the Bible. As the apostles of Jesus began to die one by one, most by martyrdom, it became clear that there was a need to preserve their teaching for the next generation. For the next two hundred years, the church worked on collecting all the writings of the Apostles that were verifiably authentic. If a particular letter or book could not be proved authentic, it was left out of the final collection since that was the only safe thing to do.

Within a few centuries of Jesus, there was a solid list of letters and books collected and bound in what we now call the New Testament. It's so important to remember that the Bible began as real people's eyewitness testimony and faith-based correspondence on what it all meant. I so badly wish that the Apostle John, or Peter, or any of the Apostles were still alive today. Since they are not, though, I'm so thankful that their teaching was left behind for us to learn and grow by.

In the next few sections, we'll explore how our Bible habits can bring about abundant life.

43

MOTIVATION

You reach for the phone. You've dialed Loola's number even before you realize what you're doing. The phone beeps about the same time you remember that Loola no longer lives in your neighborhood. You set down the phone and glance out the window.

Your eyes fall toward the kitchen sink, and across the counter where the Gardener's Almanac waits. You haven't touched the book since Loola gifted it. You move reluctantly toward the overly thick volume. It's heavy in your hand as you thumb through its pages. The words are small, and there are fewer pictures than you like. With a deep breath, you set the book down and look back through the window.

Although you recognize that there is an immense amount of knowledge to be gained in the Almanac, you can't help but resist. You don't want to read that book. You want to hear Loola's charm and wit in person.

"Come on," you say to the book. "Let's go." Gathering the Almanac, you tuck it under your arm as you pass out the back door. You spend about five minutes staring at the tree before you take a seat in Loola's old chair. You haven't had the heart to put it back in storage.

You open the Gardener's Almanac to the first page and begin with the words printed there. It's only a few sentences before you realize your eyes are moving down the page, but your mind has wandered off. Maybe I'm not supposed to start at the beginning. Flipping through the pages, you pick a chapter in the middle of the book. This time, the attempt has the same effect. The book closes with a disgruntled thump, and you head back for the house.

As you enter the kitchen door and lay the book down, you speak as if Aunt Loola is there to hear. "What's the point of reading a gardening book, anyway?"

She doesn't magically appear, so you put it out of your mind. You have other things to do, anyway. Maybe you'll find motivation later in the afternoon.

44
WHY STUDY

Why do we need Scripture? If you want to experience abundant life, you are going to need to get your mind in the right place. To maintain that fundamental mindset, you need to be taking in God's word.

The early church's believers *devoted themselves to the apostles' teaching.*[1] The Apostle's teaching is now collected in what we call the New Testament. They were committed to that teaching as a central part of their lives.

All through the New Testament, the apostles instruct believers to learn from God's word. Peter told some of his listeners when he said, *as newborn babies, desire the pure milk of the word, that you may grow thereby.*[2] Without growth, there will be no fruit.

Transformation is possible when you are aided by God's word. The fully abundant life is going to require you to engage with Scripture in some way. Whether listening, reading, or reviewing memorized passages, you need to be engaging with God's word.

This truth was explained by the writer of Hebrews. He

said, *God's word is alive and working. It is sharper than the sharpest sword and cuts all the way into us. It cuts deep to the place where the soul and the spirit are joined. God's word cuts to the center of our joints and our bones. It judges the thoughts and intentions of the heart.*[3]

Your mind is a mixture of good and bad thoughts, valuable and filthy motives, intentions both useful and detrimental. There is something magical about interacting with God's word. It can divide the useful stuff from the mess. Scripture is like a scalpel specifically designed by God to sever the thoughts and intentions that will keep you from experiencing abundant life.

On your quest to gain abundant life, you will need a regular dose of God's word. Paul put it this way, *Let the word of Christ dwell in you richly.*[4] God's word only dwells in us richly if we dwell on it regularly. For Christ's word to dwell in us richly, we need to understand what the Bible is saying.

Scripture is designed to bring abundant life, hanging like fruit-laden branches, to the average man and woman. However, that doesn't mean that everyone comes to understand what is written in the pages of Scripture. Why is it that so many people misunderstand the Bible?

The writer of Hebrews gives at least one reason when he says, *We have a great deal to say about this, and it is difficult to explain since you have become too lazy to understand. Although by this time you ought to be teachers, you need someone to teach you the basic principles of God's revelation [word] again. You need milk, not solid food.*[5]

Did you notice the phrase *too lazy to understand?* It's true that understanding God's word is going to take work. It's possible to be *too lazy to understand.* Reading the Bible isn't always easy, and so many give up. Or instead, they simply do it out of duty, not really paying attention to what they are reading.

There is another reason why many people misunderstand the truths that can be found in Scripture. They suffer from what I call the *I can do it myself,* syndrome. My three-year-old son says, "I can do it myself," quite often. In fact, many times, he will cry if someone opened his cheese stick packaging when he wanted to do it on his own. This is despite the fact that there are things he just simply can't do. He needs help.

Gaining a grasp of Scripture is not something you can do on your own. There is this amazing story in the gospels where Jesus is talking to a few of his friends. The writer says that while they talked, *He opened their minds so they could understand the Scriptures.*[6] Why would they need their minds to be opened? Didn't we say that the Scriptures are for everyone? They are, but this comes with a caveat.

We must approach the Scriptures humbly, seeking God's help to understand. We need Him to open our minds to the word. This is why I often find myself praying between the lines of my Bible, "Lord, what does this mean?" This is not so different from what the Psalm writer said when he prayed, *Give me understanding according to Your word.*[7]

Praying this kind of prayer, for understanding of Scripture, keeps my mind sharp and focused on finding the answer. Prayer is a vital part of understanding scripture. James said, *If any of you lacks wisdom, you should ask God, who gives generously to all without finding fault, and it will be given to you.*[8] If you ask for wisdom and understanding, especially concerning God's word, that is a prayer that pleases God to answer.

In addition to praying for understanding of the Scriptures, when I come to a difficult verse, I check my interpretation against other more clear verses I'm already aware of. I can't tell you how many times I've gone back to old simple favorites like John 3:16, Ephesians 2:8-9, or John 5:24.

As I check Scripture against Scripture, I also talk with trusted friends who have more Bible knowledge than I do to gain a wider perspective. I listen for answers from Bible teachers and trusted preachers. In short, even if I'm reading my Bible by myself, I'm not really studying alone.

It should be said that wisdom and understanding rarely comes in a magical moment of revelation, at least for me. I'm leary of anyone who says God spoke to them. I'm even wary of people who say God communicated to them through their impressions or feelings. What I've noticed is when I pray for understanding of Scripture, most of the time, God answers my "what does this mean?" prayer by allowing me to cross paths with a Bible teacher, or radio sermon, or preacher who answers the questions I'm looking for. That is an answer to prayer, even if it doesn't seem nearly as miraculous as lightning to the brain would. The prayer is critical, though, because it both aligns my mind with the goal of finding the answer and invites God to lead me to the place where I will find the answer.

Unfortunately, many have come up with some strange and faulty conceptions of what God is saying in the Bible because they have approached Scripture with an *I can do it on my own,* approach. Keep praying, keep believing that you can understand, and I'm convinced God will allow you to cross paths with the answer you seek.

Now, remember, we're not doing this because it's the ultimate goal. The ultimate goal is to have abundant life. We achieve abundant life by keeping a Godly mindset. Scripture study is a habit that can help us accomplish that very thing. In the next chapter, we're going to take a look at some ways to make scripture study less laborious and boring.

45
BORED

It's been days since you've worked in the garden. You peer out every time you cross the back window, but you can't make yourself walk out. Even across the lawn, you see the weeds are returning. Instead of working on the garden, you opt for a half measure. You've tried already, but you decide to double your reading efforts.

You retrieve the Gardener's Almanac from its place on the shelf. How am I going to do this? You run your finger down the table of contents. There are thirty-six chapters spread across seven hundred and fifty pages. If it were an adventure novel, you could probably get through that many words in a few weeks, but the book isn't exactly a page turner.

"I could do it in a year," you say as if there is someone to hear. "Let's see. If I could read two pages a day, I would have this fat book done before the calendar turns over."

You read, once more, on page one. It's an introduction. You learn little, but you keep driving toward your two-page goal. In less than five minutes, you've made it through. By the afternoon, you've forgotten what you read, but you remember you fulfilled your quota.

The next day, you come back to the page you marked. After straightening the dog-eared crease, you skim your two pages as your mind wanders. You hardly consider what you read, but after you're finished, you glance out the back window. "I should probably go pull some weeds."

At this moment, an odd thing crosses your mind, though you don't recognize it for its strangeness. Even though you have not been in the garden for a few days, you feel as if you've fulfilled your gardening duty. After all, you spent your time reading the gardening book. You don't go out to tend your fruit tree for the rest of the week, opting to stay in the air conditioning and read your two pages a day.

Months pass without you stepping foot in the garden. Weeds grow, vines return, and thorny branches fight with vengeance for their spare inch of sun. You miss being in your garden. The fond memories of Loola's voice mixing with the sound of the breeze plays gently in your mind. It's not just Loola you miss. It's been too long since you've been in the sunlight, the fresh air, under a big forgiving sky.

Almost without thinking, you head for the back door but stop short when you spot the Gardener's Almanac. You're at least three days behind on your reading and you promised yourself that you'd catch up before the weekend. Instead of going out to spend some quality time pulling weeds, you plop down at the kitchen table with a grunt. You find your mark in the book and let your eyes work their way down the page. You hardly pay attention to a single sentence, eagerly trying to fulfill your commitment.

After thirty minutes of bored reading, you finally rise from the chair. Your back hurts and your eyes are tired, but you're ready to get out into the garden. You head for the back door when you hear thunder. You twist and pull the doorknob right as the rain begins.

"Perfect," you say as you slam the door shut.

It isn't long before you feel trapped in a pattern of boredom and irritation. You often struggle to fulfill your reading plan. You're irritable when you have to read and sullen when you skip.

"This isn't working," you say after trying to grind through another two pages, one Friday afternoon. Reading two pages shouldn't be hard, but you just can't stand it anymore. You pick the book up and head for the trash can. Your hand hovers there for a few moments, but you can't drop it in. Even if you're not going to read it, it doesn't deserve to go in the garbage. It was a gift from Loola, after all.

"What would Loola say?" you ask. In your best imitation of her voice, you answer your own question.

"What's your gardening goal?"

"Well, it sure isn't reading two pages a day." You turn toward the door with the book in hand. You know she wouldn't let you get away without answering her question, so you pay her the honor of stating the obvious. "My gardening goal is fruit, abundant fruit."

You go for the back door and head for the garden. When you arrive, you're embarrassed at its pitiful state. You set the Gardener's Almanac on Loola's chair, which feels symbolic somehow. After getting your gloves and shovel from the garden shed, you come back and make a plan.

"Fruit, abundant fruit," you say to the weeds as you kneel and begin your work. For the next two hours, you turn the overgrown patch of land back into a respectable garden. Mostly you're using what Loola taught you, but something unexpected happens as you work.

"Nutsedge," you say as you uproot a weedy handful of

volunteer growth. You reach for another and call it by its name, "Sandbur." Another tuft of weed gets your attention. You wrap your hand around the stalk and are about to pull when a flash of memory sparks. "Oh, Lamb's-Quarter," you say.

You close your eyes, doing your best to remember something you read a few days earlier. You may want to leave Lamb's-quarter in your garden because it restores nutrients to the soil and is edible. Plucking a few seeds from the plant, you pop them into your mouth. It's no apple, but it has a bearable flavor.

"I guess I picked up a few things," you say as you sit upright and glance toward the book which now occupies Loola's honorary garden seat.

"I guess I will keep you around." you say. You're not surprised when the book doesn't respond.

46
BIBLE BOREDOM

You may have become tired of Bible reading. You may have had Bible-thumping kill-joys ram it down your throat so much that you can't stand the idea of cracking that dusty old book. Your mind might wander when you read your Bible. It might be difficult to imagine getting into the Scriptures daily, but Jesus offers a tremendous motivation for doing exactly that.

Jesus said, *those who hear the word of God and keep it are blessed!*[1] Blessed means happy. A blessed life is an abundant life. Do you want abundant life? Then you need to be spending time engaging with God's word. In this chapter, I want to help you figure out how to stay interested when you're bored to tears by your Bible.

First, you need to have the right mindset toward the purpose of Bible reading. If you turn Bible study into a check-list chore, you'll probably hate it. The goal is not to read your Bible every day for a certain amount of time. Your goal is abundant life. You want more joy, more love, more peace. Those things are supported by a Bible habit.

To get your mindset right, pray that God would give you an interest in His word. Remember, transformation power comes from God's Spirit. That Spirit was able to bring Jesus back from the dead. He's able to help you find joy in His words. Ask for a desire to study your Bible.

King David has a great prayer. He wrote about his desire to maintain a passion for God's word. You can read it by going to Psalm 119, but I'll give you a highlight reel.

He said, *my life is down in the dust; give me life through your word… I am weary from grief; strengthen me through your word… I put my hope in your word… I am afflicted very much; Revive me, O Lord, according to Your word.*[2] Toward the end of David's prayer, he said, *how sweet are Your words to my taste, Sweeter than honey to my mouth!*[3]

David prayed that God would use His word to revive, encourage, and bring hope. David understood that a more abundant life was unlocked by God's word. Do what David did, pray for passion. Pray that God would give you a David-like view of Scripture.

The second thing you can do to grow an interest in God's word is to use the Scripture as a means of fellowship. Dr. Luke tells us, *all the believers devoted themselves to the apostles' teaching, and to fellowship, and to sharing in meals (including the Lord's Supper), and to prayer.*[4]

The early believers were devoted to the Apostle's teaching, in other words, the Bible. However, they didn't go off and study the Scriptures on their own. Instead, they shared and talked about what God had told his people. They engaged with God's word in the context of fellowship. This is one of the greatest tools you can use to become more excited about God's word.

You need to find other people that are excited about Scripture and spend time with them. If you're bored by your Bible, it might be because you've only spent time with people who are also bored with their Bibles, or worse, they use their Bibles as a means to be legalistic. Learning from God's word in a group of trusted believers, especially under the direction of an exciting teacher, is a way to leave the dry desert and enter a lush land of learning.

Notice how Paul explains the relationship between Scripture and social encouragement. He says, *Let the word of Christ dwell in you richly in all wisdom, teaching and admonishing one another.*[5] Part of letting the word of God dwell in us richly is by being encouraged and taught by one another. God's word is meant to be shared.

There is another tool that Paul mentions in the verse. *Admonishing one another in psalms and hymns and spiritual songs, singing with grace in your hearts to the Lord.*[6] In addition to studying the word with other believers, rather than alone, he says that we should be *singing* the Word of God. We should be taught and encouraged by songs that are based on Scripture.

For years I was on the other end of the spectrum. I grumpily resisted singing songs in church. I wasn't in a good place spiritually. I'd sit sourly and stare at the words, not even mouthing them. I was disobeying the verse. Things began changing for me a number of years ago. As I've worked to spend more time with my mind on Godly things, I recognize that one great way to do this is to sing along with songs that are based on Scripture.

There's another kind of Bible song that doesn't make it to the radio or into popular playlists. It's what I call word-for-word Bible songs. There are lots of word-for-word Bible songs for kids. If you do a little digging, you can find some high-quality ones for adults as well.[7] Songs like this can make you *feel something* while you listen to God's word… no reading required.

There are lots of people that just don't read books. They certainly don't read books as thick as the Bible. The idea of picking up the Bible is daunting enough, but how much more for someone who doesn't enjoy reading. This brings me to my next suggestion.

My father-in-law loves to work in his shop. Just about anytime he's working alone, he has an audiobook version of the Bible playing. Whether he's welding, slicing boards, or fixing an old rocking chair, he's also listening to the Bible. I have another friend who listens to an audiobook version of the Bible while he exercises. He's improving his physical and spiritual fitness at the same time. There's a guy who is a truck driver; he has listened through the Bible so many times while driving he can't count. This is a great option for anyone who feels intimidated by reading.

If you're struggling to be interested in God's word, here are my suggestions. First, remember that your ultimate goal is not to read a certain amount of your Bible each day or year. Your ultimate goal is to have abundant life, and Scripture is a helpful tool to allow you to achieve that. Second, pray that God will give you a passion for His word. Third, study your Bible with other trustworthy people who are excited about it. Finally, try Scripture in other formats like music and audiobooks.

As you seek to find abundance in God's word, I'm confident He will provide the interest and passion you need to stay engaged. Remember, abundant life is waiting! In the next chapter, we are going to discover the transforming power of God's word.

47

FEED THE TREE

You've caught up with the weeding duties and the garden is back on track. Loola's chair sits open at the edge of your one tree orchard. For now, your tree is doing well, but you feel as if there are probably things you ought to be doing to ensure its health.

You plop down in Loola's old garden side seat and begin to thumb through the pages of the gardening almanac. You have changed the way you interact with the book. You usually read a little from it each day, but you're not on a schedule. Your reading comes naturally, since hardly a day goes by that you don't have some question you'd like answered. Since you don't have Loola, you consult the book.

It doesn't take long before you recognize a question forming in your mind. You thumb toward the section you're looking for. Another few seconds, and you locate the portion on fruit trees. You run your finger down the page and discover a chapter titled "Feeding Your Fruit Tree." Like a hound dog on a scent, you chase down the page number and begin following the trail. The voice of your inner-monologue, verbalizing the text, is Aunt Loola's.

Although you already had a vague sense of what the tree needs, it comes into focus as you read. Feeding the tree requires watering and fertilizing. You quickly discover that it's not yet time of season to fertilize, so you focus on the trees watering needs. You discover that if the tree has too much water, whatever grows will wilt prematurely, and the leaves will be yellow and brittle. If you underwater the tree, its canopy will be unhealthy and won't support the fruiting process. If you get it wrong in either direction, you won't have fruit.

But how can you know how much is enough? You let your eyes drink in the words as you skim down the page. A small paragraph near the bottom reveals the answer. You have to check the soil. It instructs the conscientious arborist to take a long screwdriver and plunge it into the soil near the base of the tree. If it is difficult to push the screwdriver into the soil, then give the tree a drink. If the screwdriver glides into the soil and doesn't feel firmly held in one place, then there is too much water. Since this test is easy, you can do it often. The last line of the paragraph catches your attention. It was not long ago that you heard Loola say these exact words.

"Water the soil, not the tree," the Almanac warns. It's as if Loola's own words echo through the air. You read on as the warm wash of reminiscence cascades over you.

The Gardener's Almanac offers a more thorough test that can be done occasionally. It gives instructions to dig down six to eight inches and retrieve a handful of soil. It should be moist and cool. If it crumbles, the tree needs more water; if it's soggy mud, the tree needs less.

You lay the book on the garden chair, rush to your shed, and get the needed implements. In another few seconds, you're on your knees examining the dirt. Within a minute, you know what you need to do.

48
TRANSFORMED BY SCRIPTURE

To have abundant life, you need transformation. Transformation happens when your mind is set on things above. Studying God's word gives you the thoughts you need to stay focused upon. When you're mindset is right, God grows spiritual fruit in you. As the fruits of the Spirit grow inside you, there is less soil for sin to take seed. Thus you are transformed.

In talking about this concept, King David said, *I have stored up your word in my heart, that I might not sin against you.*[1] David's goal was to have a heart and mind so packed with God's word that it transformed his actions. Remember, the key to transformation is where your mind is set. If your mind is full of Scripture, there will hardly be any room for a flesh-powered approach.

I think this is why Paul once said to his star student, Timothy, that there were those who *resist the truth" and thus have "corrupt minds.*[2] The truth of God's word needs to work its way into our minds in one way or another. If we resist taking in the truth of Scripture, then we can expect to have our mindset fall back to that old default, the flesh.

That's why Paul goes on to say, *All Scripture is given by God. And all Scripture is useful for teaching and for showing people what is wrong in their lives. It is useful for correcting faults and teaching the right way to live. Using the Scriptures, those who serve God will be prepared and will have everything they need to do every good work.*[3]

If you rely on the Spirit and use the Scriptures as your guide, you have what you need to succeed in the Christian life. If you intend to serve God as you study the Scripture, it will drive you toward a Spiritual mindset. It will lead you to a place where you not only think Spiritual thoughts but good deeds will grow out of the spiritual thoughts. That's where the fruit is.

Paul once said that he wanted his friends to *Walk worthy of the Lord, fully pleasing Him, being fruitful in every good work and increasing in the knowledge of God.*[4] Fruit is an analogy for good works. There is a relationship between a growing Godly knowledge and the ability to do good works. This knowledge must come from God's word. The knowledge you get from Scripture strengthens your ability to do good works, which is bearing fruit. Once again, transformed life comes from your engagement with Scripture and the resulting mindset.

In another letter, Paul said, *And we all, who with unveiled faces contemplate the Lord's glory, are being transformed into his image with ever-increasing glory, which comes from the Lord, who is the Spirit.*[5]

Transformation occurs when you contemplate, which is another word for setting your mind on, the Lord's glory. When you simply think about God and Godly things, something happens. You are mysteriously being transformed into a person that looks a little more like Jesus. This isn't by your power of will, determination, or grit. It's accomplished by the power of the Spirit that is inside you. Now, this raises an obvious question. Where do the concepts you should contemplate come from? Scripture!

You need to fill your thought tank with Spiritual concepts to contemplate. You do this by engaging with the Word of God. Now, it's important to note that one can fill their mind with facts but never really contemplate those facts. If you read your Bible, constantly gaining knowledge, but never contemplate the implications of what you learn, then you're missing out on the transformation. You're leaving a feast on the table untasted. It's when you take in God's word but also focus on its meaning that the transformation begins to occur. It's sad to think about how many people are mechanically reading God's word but never spending a moment to consider its implications.

When we contemplate those high concepts, like God's Glory, it's like we are staring into the radiant majesty without anything to cover our faces. Moses was transformed into a glowy-faced guy when he entered the presence of the Lord. When we contemplate things we've learned in Scripture, we, too, are transformed. When you focus on God, the Spirit works on your flesh to bring it in alignment with righteous living.

Your ultimate goal is not to become a person who reads their Bible for a certain amount of time each day. You could read it for hours a day and still miss the point. You need to become a person that longs for the transformation the Spirit offers so that you can live an abundant life. That desire for transformation, and a deep-seated wish for the abundant life that comes with it, can drive you to the pages of Scripture.

Such love, joy, peace will well up from your time in prayer and in the word that you can't stand to go too long without it.

There is one more major category of helpful habits that we will examine in the next section.

PART V
FELLOWSHIP

49

FELLOWSHIP

You've pulled the weeds. You've cut out the thorns. You've mulched, watered, and fertilized at the right time of the season for a few years now. Since Aunt Loola's departure, you've done everything you could to bring the tree to fruition. Your tree looks like a formidable teen should; for a few seasons now, it has appeared as if it could blossom with abundance. Each season, however, it barely buds with anything sweet. A few stray fruits hang from the branches, but this isn't the abundance your mouth has been watering for for years.

As another season passes, you're discouraged to find that, while it's getting taller, it still isn't producing the way it should. As you've done so many times since Loola left, you retrieve the copy of The Gardener's Almanac that she gave you. You knock the soil from its covers and thumb through the well-worn pages. You've read most of the book, many parts multiple times. As you scan the pages, you look for any information that might give you a clue as to why your tree isn't producing a better crop.

Somewhere in the middle portion of the volume, you find a note explaining an important aspect of the plant life in your garden. It reads, "This kind of fruit tree must be pollinated by other fruit trees in order to grow fruit. For best practice, plant a variety of fruit trees nearby."

It had not occurred to you that other fruit trees would be required in order to bring in a sizable crop. You're small garden only has room for one tree, but you glance at an overgrown plot of ground next door. It resides squarely within your neighbor's property tucked into the vine-covered, forgotten stretch of his narrow backyard.

"Hello, neighbor," you say one afternoon. You've timed your trip to the mailbox to coincide with Lenard's. It's taken you a few weeks to get up the nerve to broach the subject with him, but as soon as the words are out of your mouth, his warm smile washes away all of your nervousness.

He's a gregarious man who works nights. Saturdays, he works in the yard and spends time with his family. You've greeted him several times before but never shared much more than small talk.

“Hey,” Lenard says. “How’s that fruit tree coming?”

“It’s growing,” you say. Lenard has his mail in hand now and is already moving toward his front door. You start moving in his direction. “Hey, that reminds me, there’s something I wanted to ask you about.” You close the distance between and meet him at the edge of your front yard.

“What’s up?” Lenard says. “Did my kid kick his ball into your backyard again? I’ve told him to be careful.”

"No—" you say. "Well, yeah, but I just kicked it back. It wasn't a big deal."

“Oh, good.”

"So, as you know, I have this fruit tree—" you pause long enough for him to respond.

"Yeah, I'm jealous. I wish I had a green thumb like yours," Lenard says.

You hold up your hand, showing off the color of your digits. "No green thumb, they're just human colored," you say, remembering the time Loola had said the same. You're glad Lenard smiles at the silly joke. "But that's kind of what I wanted to talk to you about."

"Really?"

"Yeah, so, I'm still learning how to take care of a tree, actually," you say. "It turns out that some particular kinds of fruit trees need to be pollinated by other fruit trees."

"I'm guessing yours is one of those *particular kinds*?" Lenard guesses.

"Yep," you say. "But I don't have enough space in my backyard to plant another one. And as far as I know, there aren't any other fruit trees around here." You are about to ply your request, but Lenard beats you to it.

"I'd be happy to plant one in my backyard," he says. "Would that be close enough?"

"Absolutely," you say with a wide grin. You could hug the man, but you refrain.

"The only problem is, I'll probably kill it," Lenard says. "I'm not all that good with growing things. And I don't know how to get started. I mean, do I just drop a seed in the ground, or— I mean— I—"

"Hey, what would you think of me helping you out?" you ask. "I could pop in every once in a while and share what I know. It isn't much, but maybe together, we could get it off to a good start."

Lenard lights up like a Christmas tree. "That would be great!" he says. He gestures to the house and says, "Beth will be so excited; she loves fruit. And I'd love for my kids to learn how to grow stuff too."

"This will be fun," you say, genuinely reflecting his excitement.

"I'm free on Saturdays," he says. "Would that work?"

"That's perfect."

50
ABUNDANCE IN FELLOWSHIP

Many fruit trees must be cross pollinated. Most can't pollinate if they are isolated. What's interesting is that many fruit trees do not have to be pollinated by other trees exactly like themselves. They need a variety. If there are other compatible varieties of fruit trees nearby that bloom at the time they can cross pollinate and produce fruit.

Christians are somewhat similar. If you isolate from other believers, like a lone fruit tree, it's going to be extremely hard to grow the kind of spiritual fruit God wants to produce in your life. So many people say, "I don't want to go to that church because there is no one like *me* there." Remember, trees don't need other trees like themselves. It takes a variety to grow fruit.

The ultimate goal of your time here is not to become someone that attends church on a regular basis. That would be a disappointing goal. Your ultimate goal is to experience abundant life. You're goal, in other words, is to bear an abundance of Spiritual fruit like love, joy, peace, and the like. The analogy of the fruit tree reminds us that believers need other believers to bear fruit. That is at least in part, because so much of the Spiritual fruit, has to do with other people. The Christian life is not meant to be spent alone. We are fellowship fruit trees.

The author of Hebrews put it this way, *We should think about each other to see how we can encourage each other to show love and do good works. We must not quit meeting together, as some are doing. No, we need to keep on encouraging each other. This becomes more and more important as you see the Day getting closer.*[1]

That encourages us to fellowship, and tells us why we should. When faithful believers get together their goal is to stir up love and good works. Remember, Paul called good works "fruit" and love is one of the fruits of the Spirit. Your ultimate goal is to have that fruitful and abundant life we've been talking about. Fellowship with other committed believers is one of the main ways to experience it.

Love is one of the fruits of the Spirit.[2] Love comes from God. In fact, you're not able to love in a way that pleases Him, unless you are both born again, and walking with Him.[3] It's possible to be born again, but not be obeying his commandment to love one another. That's why the Bible is so packed with instructions on loving one another. To love one another we must get in close proximity.

Not only is there greater love to be had in fellowship, but there is joy. Notice how John put it when he said, *We want you to have fellowship with us. The fellowship we share together is with God the Father and his Son Jesus Christ. We write these things to you so that you can be full of joy with us.*[4]

When we have fellowship with other believers, and when that fellowship is rooted in our relationship with God the Father, and Jesus His Son, there is joy. Actually John says that we can be *full of joy!* Doesn't that sound like abundant life?

That's your ultimate goal. That means you're going to need to experience fellowship in some way.

We've seen *love*, *joy*, but is there *peace* in fellowship? Think of what Paul said to his friends in Philippi. *make my joy complete: Agree with each other, and show your love for each other. Be united in your goals and in the way you think.*[5] Paul's instruction is to treat each other in alignment with all of the fruits of the Spirit. In his words I see *love, joy, peace, patience, kindness, goodness, gentleness,* and *self-control.* When we experience quality Christian fellowship, we experience a piece of the abundant life we are designed for. When we couple our fellowship with the private spiritual life that we've been talking about, life can become fully abundant.

When you're a scripture-studying, prayer-reliant person in private, then fellowship with other faithful believers is where the abundant life is most intensely experienced. Fellowship is where it all comes together. Without fellowship of believers, you're missing a huge portion of the Christian experience.

Years ago I was taught a pretty surprising lesson from an unexpected place. I met a Christian singer, who was anything but traditional looking. He played loud rock music, and had the longest beard I'd ever seen. He had tattoos and earrings. Despite his look, he was an outspoken witness for the Lord on stage and off. He spent much of his time playing in little dive bars around the south. He had not found any measure of fame, but his music was good, and he talked about Christ everywhere he went.

After one of his shows I caught up with him next to the stage. I found myself complaining about my church, and expressing my bitterness toward other believers who I attended with. I told him I was interested in starting a church because everyone I knew where I went was so hypocritical. I figured he could understand. After all, he must be an outcast looking the way he did. I was surprised how he responded.

"I hear what you're saying, man, but I have to disagree," he said gently and with real kindness. "I have a church. It's a bunch of white haired old people and me. They love me, and I love them. I don't look like them, but they don't care. They do church just like they did in 1954. Most would say the church is dying, but I feel the most alive when I'm there. I've found more joy at that little place. It's my home." He knelt to put away a guitar cable as he continued. "I don't want to go to church with people just like me. I want to go to church with people who can love me despite our differences. That's real fellowship, man."

I was jealous of his church. Actually, no that's not right. I was jealous of the abundant life he was experiencing. He was feeling what John talked about, being full of joy by fellowship. I'll never forget the lesson he taught me.

I think this is why Jesus said, *For where two or three are gathered together in My name, I am there in the midst of them.*[6] Jesus loves our fellowship, shouldn't we love it too? If you want to be where Jesus is, gather with His people.

Have you been tempted to isolate from other believers? Have you found it hard to fellowship at times? I know that I have, but I keep coming back because there is abundant life waiting in the midst of any group who meets in Jesus' name. Certainly this doesn't mean that every time we meet together is sweet, easy, or pleasant. In an upcoming chapter we'll talk about how to turn meetings into fellowship.

51

HELPER

When Saturday comes around, you are ready. You are knocking on Lenard's door as soon as the sun is up. He comes to the front dressed in overalls and looks as if he's ready to work.

"Good morning," you say. "I'm looking forward to planting that tree."

"Oh, yeah." His tone of voice leaves you in doubt.

"Do you still want to?"

"For sure," Lenard says. He rubs the back of his neck and looks at the ground. "It's just that my car is broken. I only have today to fix it. I'm really sorry. Could we do it next week?"

"No problem," you say. You hide your disappointment well. As you walk back to your house, you stop by the shed and drop off your gloves and tools. Standing in the doorway, you do a quick personal pep talk and head into the house.

It feels like the week is taking forever to finish. When Saturday finally comes back around, you're up bright and early once again. This time you call first, preferring to spare the embarrassment you likely caused Lenard the previous week. The phone rings a handful of times, but Lenard doesn't pick up. You set your phone down and look out the side window.

"Oh, there he is," you say. He's standing on a ladder that is leaned up against the side of his house. You pour out the back door and make your way to the edge of your yard.

"Hey, neighbor," you say. Even with your hand shielding your eyes, you still have to squint. Lenard half turns and looks down.

"Hey." Lenard comes down and stands awkwardly by the foot of the ladder. "Listen. I know I said we could plant that tree today, but I've got some rotten boards on the house that I have to replace."

"That's ok," you say. This time you're feeling a little hurt. "You think we might try to do it next Saturday?"

"That would be great."

You head back into your house and watch Lenard nailing the boards up. You check on him every few hours, hoping he will finish in enough time to work in the garden, but he's out until it's dark.

The following week feels like a month. You decide you'll give it one more try, but if he's too busy, then you'll stop pestering him.

You ring his doorbell at seven in the morning. He has his work overalls on again, which is a good sign, but he has a pipe wrench in his left hand, which isn't.

"Feel like doing some gardening?"

"That sounds great. I wish I could," he says. Your eyes go to the red handled tool he's gripping. He holds it up when he notices you looking. "Yeah, I've got a clogged toilet. I started taking things apart last night, and it's looking like an all-day job."

"No problem," you say, but your words don't match your

emotion. You don't try to arrange for the next Saturday. What's the point? You step off his porch and walk toward your house.

"Hey," you say as an idea sparks. "Can I help you with your plumbing?"

"That's nice, but you don't have to do that."

You come back up the porch feeling a spring in your step. "Maybe with the both of us on the job, we can make quick work of it."

"Are you sure? It's a mess."

"Positive." He smiles and lets you in. As you enter the house, you spot a woman sitting on the couch, crossed legged and tapping her toe on the floor. Lenard points with the wrench. "Have you met Beth, my wife?"

"Nice to meet you," you say.

"She's pretty eager for me to get our bathroom back together," Lenard says. "Clock's ticking." He smiles awkwardly and turns to go down the hall. You take a second to realize what Lenard means.

"Oh," you say. "You can use my restroom. My house is unlocked. No one is home." Beth rises immediately and steps forward.

"Seriously?" she says. Without waiting for a response, she moves toward the front door. "Thank you so much. I was panicking."

In the hall, you glance into a room decorated for kids. "That's Josh and Andrew," Lenard says. Two young boys wave and say hi as you pass. You greet them and follow Lenard into the small single sized bathroom.

Plumbing parts are all over the floor, some broken. You survey the damage and get ready to work. As you look around Lenard says, "Honestly, I don't know what I'm doing." After a few minutes of studying the problem, you stand upright.

"It looks like your s-trap is clear and there's no hard water build up on the drain lines. Have you checked the tank volume?"

"Like I said," Lenard reiterates, "I don't know much about plumbing."

"Here I'll show you." You show him how the float valve works and explain how to adjust the tank volume. "Since there are no other problems that we know of, we just need to put everything back together and try it out."

"Where'd you learn this stuff?" Lenard asks. "You a plumber or something?"

"Nah, just kind of picked it up over the years, I guess." You help him reattach all the threaded pipe fittings around the sink. There's no reason he had to dismantle them, but you don't say so. In a few minutes, you have the water back on, and the toilet works perfectly. By now, Beth is back and extremely thankful.

Now that his task is complete, Lenard gladly shows you to his backyard where you plan out the fruit garden with him. His wife and boys come out and join in the conversation. You feel great having served them. You can sense a genuine bond growing.

52

FELLOWSHIP BY SERVICE

It's possible to go to meetings but not have fellowship. *Fellowship* in the original language of the Bible basically means "sharing." In talking about the early church, some Bible translations say, "They devoted themselves to... *fellowship,*" while others use the phrase, *They shared everything they had.*[1] So fellowship means to share what you have.

Often, we think of modern church fellowship as sitting around and talking about our feelings. If that's what you think of as fellowship, then you're missing out on a huge aspect of this Christian concept. In fact, if you think of fellowship as just talking a lot, then you may not like fellowship all that much.

So, how do we turn bland meetings into fellowship? The answer is the same thing I tell my kids all the time, "share." Obviously, sharing will include talking, but it's much more than that. About the first generation of the church, Luke said, *The whole group of believers was united in their thinking and in what they wanted. None of them said that the things they had were their own. Instead, they shared everything.*[2]

What an amazing experience that must have been. Believers are expected to share whatever is needed with each other. Fellowship is when we take care of one another. We are expected to be good to all people, but especially good to our Christian brothers and sisters. That's why Paul said, *Therefore, as we have opportunity, let us do good to all, especially to those who are of the household of faith.*[3]

Fellowship doesn't mean *only* sharing monetary resources. In fact, we all have a lot more to share than just money. Things a group of believers can share also include their time, experiences, talent, love, service, and much more. I want to focus on that last aspect for a moment. Not only are we told to share ourselves with other believers, but we are instructed to serve.

To a group of believers in Corinth, Paul said, *serve each other with love.*[4] When you serve a person, that means you love them. To love someone means to serve them. You can't disconnect these ideas. John expressed a similar idea when he said, *This is the teaching you have heard from the beginning: We must love each other.*[5] The church will be functioning most successfully, in God's eyes, when it is full of people who love one another. You can recognize the exchange of love in a group of believers because they will be serving one another.

Many might be tempted to think; *I don't like this church because no one serves me.* That's the wrong mentality. If you find yourself bored with church, or Bible study, or believer's meetings of any kind, there is a question you ought to ask yourself. You should say, "How can *I* serve these people in a way that would bring me joy?" When you begin serving others, things will change. This is especially true when you serve other believers with your own talents and spiritual gifts.

My spiritual gift, as far as I can tell, is teaching. I have some God-given ability in this area. What's amazing to me is that the thing I'm good at is also the thing I love doing. Serving other believers with this gift is a blessing to me. I feel abundant life happening when I get the chance to teach.

One of my spiritual gifts IS NOT administration. Not long ago, I was beginning to struggle with some of my own limitations. At the church where I used to serve as teaching pastor, I felt as if my lack of administrative skills was hurting the church. I sensed imminent failure was just around the corner. Trying to do administrative tasks brought stress, and was hard for me to call my feelings on the subject a blessing.

Beautifully, one of the elders, who is also a former pastor, asked me to get together for coffee. He told me that he wanted to take on an administrative role. I can't tell you how happy this made me. After bringing it to the elder board, we hired him as the administrative pastor. He is a natural planner and organizer. He occasionally taught, which he is great at, but primarily he handled administrative issues. I occasionally administered, which I'm not so good at, but primarily I handled the teaching tasks. I got to serve the congregation with my gifts, he got to serve the congregation with his gifts, and we both felt blessed to do so.

Paul lays out how we ought to use our spiritual gifts to serve one another. He says, *We all have different gifts... Whoever has the gift of prophecy should use that gift... Whoever has the gift of serving should serve. Whoever has the gift of teaching should teach. Whoever has the gift of comforting others should do that. Whoever has the gift of giving to help others should give generously. Whoever has the gift of leading should work hard at it. Whoever has the gift of showing kindness to others should do it gladly.*[6]

He expects people to stay in their lane. Why, because using your gifts bring you joy. It's an amazing feeling to use what I'm good at and enjoy doing to serve others. Paul goes on to explain what kind of experience will be shared when we use our God-given spiritual gifts to serve each other.

He says, *Your love must be real... Love each other in a way that makes you feel close, like brothers and sisters. And give each other more honor than you give yourself. As you serve the Lord, work hard and don't be lazy. Be excited about serving him!... Share with God's people who need help. Look for people who need help and welcome them into your homes.*[7]

Those instructions are laced with expressions of joy. I once had a pastor who often said, "as we serve the Lord and others, we should be moving toward destination joy." He said this to my dad, who was leading music at the time. Dad was burned out on having to lead worship every Sunday as a volunteer. My dad eventually came to the conclusion that he wasn't leading music because it brought him joy; he was doing it because he felt too guilty to admit he wanted to quit. That wise pastor talked with him about it and meant what he said. He encouraged Dad to quit and pursue other things. Now, we often sit around the living room playing music at Dad's house. He loves it, and he couldn't be happier not to be leading music at church.

Have you resisted serving other believers? Have you ever used your spiritual gifts, enthusiasms, and talents you're passionate about to serve others? This is a big part of experiencing abundant life. There is a place for everyone to serve in the body of Christ.

In the next section we'll discuss another important aspect of fellowship.

53

GRAFTING

"Pretty much all fruit trees use the same rootstock," you say as you dig your hands into the soil of Lenard's backyard.

"What does that mean?"

"When I planted my tree," you say with a laugh, "I didn't know what I was doing. I just dropped a seed in the ground and hoped it would grow."

"It looks like it worked."

"It did, but it's taking a long time for it to produce mature fruit," you explain. "What more experienced growers do is take a rootstock from an established tree and graft a bud into it."

"Why?"

"The bud they graft determines the kind of fruit you will get. You choose the rootstock based on how it does in the soil and how well it supports certain kinds of growth."

"So, that's what we're doing here?" Lenard asks.

"Yeah, I got the rootstock at the nursery. We're going to graft a scion from my tree and plant it."

"I'll pay you back for what you spent. How much do I owe you?"

"Not a chance," you say. "It's a free gift."

"Thanks!"

You reach for the pot with the rootstock and roll it across the ground to loosen the soil. You gently pull and the burgeoning sapling comes loose. You show Lenard how to remove it from its potting and place it in the ground.

"Now we're going to do a tongue and whip graft." You show him how to use the grafting knife and tape. He fumbles with it a little before he gets it right, but you're patient with him. Once he's made the cuts, you show him how to wrap it with the binding.

"Alright," you say as you stand and look down at the tree. "It's planted."

"So that branch we grafted in was from your tree?" Lenard asks.

"Yeah. This way, they can pollinate each other directly. Plus, we'll be growing the same kind of fruit."

"Can we graft other kinds of trees too?"

"Sure, as the tree grows, we could graft in other types. We could have a dozen different varieties of fruit on the same tree," you say.

"What happens if they don't pollinate each other?" Lenard asks.

"Look at my tree," you say and turn your head. "You're looking at it."

"Wow! I didn't know they needed each other so much."

"Yeah, trees have to work together to make fruit."

54
TRANSFORMED BY FELLOWSHIP

The ultimate goal of your life is to experience abundant life in the Lord. To have that kind of life, you will need to be transformed. Prayer has a transformative effect, as does Scripture study. However, if you isolate yourself from other believers, you will be missing a piece of that fruitful experience. God uses our social environment to transform us. When you are an active part of a healthy Christian fellowship, you are being transformed. In the same way that trees need each other to produce fruit, so do people. If you want abundant life, you need other Christians involved.

Paul said as much when he explained, *You, my brothers and sisters, were called to be free. But do not use your freedom to indulge the flesh; rather, serve one another humbly in love.*[1] Each person who has believed in Jesus for everlasting life has that free, irrevocable gift forever. That means that you are free. Notice what Paul says you are free to do. You are free to either *indulge the flesh* or *serve one another humbly in love.*

Paul paints these ideas as opposites. It seems, on the face of it, that you would be able to indulge the flesh while also serving in humility and love. However, you can't do both simultaneously. They are opposed to each other. One is done by the flesh; the other is powered by the Spirit.

If you are doing fellowship in a Christ-like manner, it will drown out certain desires to indulge your flesh, allowing you to set your mind in a better place while you serve. This is why it's good to go to church, but it's great to serve other believers at church and away.

Certainly, you can't be around Christians every moment of the day, but think about it, aren't you less likely to commit your favorite sins when you're around other faithful believers? Remember, it's the Spirit that transforms you, but it seems that God uses fellowship with others to play a role in that transformation. If you isolate from God's people, you are isolating from one of God's methods of bringing about abundant life.

Many people quote the author of Hebrews as telling believers that they should not be "neglecting to meet together." However, he gives a powerful reason for meeting together. He says, *let us consider how to stir up one another to love and good works, not neglecting to meet together, as is the habit of some, but encouraging one another, and all the more as you see the Day drawing near.*[2]

We aren't encouraged to meet together so that we can check off our church attendance quota. We're told to meet together so that we can stir up love and good works in each other. We are supposed to get together so we can encourage one another. We are supposed to gather so we can talk about how Jesus is going to come back one day, possibly soon. We shouldn't neglect our meetings because if we stop coming, we miss out on all of this.

The greatest experience of abundance, a life filled with fruit, is going to be lived out in fellowship with others who are encouraging us in the right direction. What's more, you are supposed to do the same for others. When you skip the fellowship, there is someone that needed encouragement from you. There is someone that needs to be motivated to love and to do good works. That's your job. When you serve other believers by encouraging them, it will open the doors for the Spirit to transform you.

Sin is a deceiver. It hardens us. We need help from each other. That's why the same author wrote, *but encourage each other daily, while it is still called today so that none of you is hardened by sin's deception.*[3] Notice that the encouragement we experience from each other is supposed to be happening daily. That means that we are expected to have more than a once-a-week relationship with other believers. Certainly, you won't be texting everyone from your church every day, but there are probably at least a few people that you could be connecting with on a daily basis. They need you, and you need them. Don't miss out.

Although it may be hard to imagine, what if you fell into the trap that sin set? What if you began to be hardened by the deception of sin? What if you start to question your faith? I know many to whom this has happened.

James offers a very social remedy when he says, *my brothers and sisters if one of you should wander from the truth and someone should bring that person back, remember this: Whoever turns a sinner from the error of their way will save them from death and cover over a multitude of sins.*[4]

There are times when you are going to need someone to steer you back to the light. There are times when you may not be seeing things correctly. If you have evacuated and isolated, then it's going to be hard for anyone to know how to help you. This is why it's so important that you plant yourself right in the middle of a vibrant fellowship.

Your ultimate goal is to experience the abundant life God has for you. To do that, you will need to be transformed. One of the places the Spirit performs that transformation is through Christian fellowship. If you run from the church, you are escaping from one of God's vehicles that can bring you to abundant life.

Remember this proverb as you consider how you will fellowship. *One who isolates himself pursues selfish desires; he rebels against all sound wisdom.*[5] Your life goal is abundant fruit. You will get there by setting your mind in the right place. The tools you use to align your mind are prayer, scripture, and as we've seen in this section, fellowship.

55
LENARD'S TREE

For five Saturdays in a row, you've spent about an hour working side by side with Lenard to prepare his garden. It is exciting to walk through the steps with him, the same steps which Loola taught you. Though it was fun to learn them from her, you had no idea how exciting it would be to share them with others.

Lenard is a quick learner. His fruit tree takes root and begins to reach for the sky. A few more months of instruction, and the balance begins to change. You're learning a lot from each other. Within six months, Lenard involves his wife in the gardening. She is a natural. They make an amazing gardening team. You always look forward to your time with Lenard and his family as you all strive toward the ultimate goal.

A year, then two more have passed. The time together strengthens your friendship with Lenard, his wife Beth, and their three kids. You're no longer just gardening together, but spending free time as an honorary member of their family. You and Lenard's family decide to tear down the fence between your back yards. This opens up the space in an amazing way.

The two fruit trees reflect the fellowship you share. Through the season, you see bees and butterflies flitting between the two trees, a good sign that pollination is taking place. The shade of the two trees is a gathering place for your new circle of beloved neighbors. You, affectionately and somewhat ironically, decide to call the unified backyard *The Orchard.*

"Lenard, Beth, have you guys seen the Orchard," you say as you knock on their back door one sunny Saturday morning. They come out quickly to the scene that awaits. Lenard gasps.

"No, way!" Lenard says, bubbling with enthusiasm. "Look at that, Honey!"

"Wow!" Beth says. "Hey, Kids, come and see."

The two trees are teeming with color and life. Hanging from what seems to be a thousand branches are budding sprouts. As you approach the tree with the family, you all examine the branches with wonder. You have a good feeling. This is going to be the year you finally get fruit, abundant fruit.

56
BRINGING OTHERS IN

Many cringe when they are told to evangelize. I want to demystify evangelism and help you see a path toward evangelism that makes sense.

Step one is to attend a church that clearly expresses the saving message of Jesus. Many churches fall woefully short of clarity on this topic. However, if you trust the leadership of your church to share the gospel with newcomers, then evangelism can be as simple as inviting outsiders into the fellowship. If you don't trust your church leadership to share the gospel, this same concept could work for a small group Bible study led by someone who clearly shares the gospel. If you don't have a clear-gospel sharing group of any kind, then you might have to modify the following ideas to fit your situation.

Jesus said that *people don't light a lamp and put it under a basket, but on a stand, and it gives light to all in the house. In the same way, let your light shine before others, so that they may see your good works and give glory to your Father who is in heaven.*[1]

There is a difference between allowing people to see your fruit and trying to produce fruit so that people can see. You are to live out your abundant life in such a way that it draws others to the orchard. Show strangers love. Talk about your joy to outsiders. Demonstrate peace in adversity. Serve people that don't deserve it and won't be able to pay you back. It's important not to do these things for the sake of pride, but it's ok to allow others to see your good works as well.

When people see your good works, your love for one another, your peace with each other, and your joy in fellowship, others will glorify God. This is a way of attracting outsiders into the fellowship. When you do this, it is a great setup for evangelism.

One powerful tool in evangelism is to be part of a loving group of believers. This starts with a simple concept. A fellowship of believers should be a very inviting place. Note what Jesus said, *By this, all will know that you are My disciples if you have love for one another.*[2] The world is a savage and dangerous place. It's full of vengeance, rivalry, and spite. Any group of ordinary people is going to experience these negative aspects. So a group of people who genuinely love one another is unique in this fallen world. So unique, in fact, that Jesus promises that people will see the difference when you love one another. They will be able to recognize Jesus' power at work in that group.

Believers should, *Therefore welcome one another as Christ has welcomed you, for the glory of God.*[3] When someone new comes to a church, Bible study, or gathering, they ought to be welcomed as if it were Jesus Himself welcoming them. When a new person is invited and welcomed to take part in a gathering of believers, especially one who shares the saving message on a regular basis, evangelism will happen naturally. The newcomer will hear the gospel by simply being present. This is why it's important to be welcoming and be part of a group that shares a clear gospel on a regular basis.

I think this organic style of evangelism is what Jesus had in mind when he said, *Make disciples of all nations, baptizing them in the name of the Father and of the Son and of the Holy Spirit, teaching them to observe all that I have commanded you. And behold, I am with you always, to the end of the age.*[4]

Jesus doesn't say to evangelize people in this famous passage. Discipleship is a separate thing from salvation.[5] Instead, it's assumed evangelism will happen as people come in contact with groups of believers. Evangelism can happen in a very short amount of time, whereas discipleship should last for the rest of a person's life.

So, the concept that you need to share your faith doesn't need to be as intimidating as you might have once thought. It can be as simple as inviting a person to take part in a gospel-sharing fellowship of believers. As you do that, questions might come up. Of course, Peter said, *always being prepared to make a defense to anyone who asks you for a reason for the hope that is in you, yet do it with gentleness and respect.*[6]

Notice that Peter's instructions are not to force people to listen to answers for which they asked no question. Instead, we are to be prepared to answer questions that come up. It's more than passive but less than forceful. Notice the final words he uses. These answers should be given with gentleness and respect.

So, we invite new people into our gospel-sharing fellowship, we work to be welcoming, and we ready ourselves to answer any questions they have.

There are many who are not able to attend a church that shares a clear saving message on a regular basis. If that's the case, the above method may fall flat. In fact, I'd be hesitant to invite a new believer to a church that shares a convoluted or confusing gospel message. There are plenty of them out there. If that is the case with your church, you might have to simply do what Paul told his star student Timothy, *do the work of an evangelist.*[7] This might include starting a small group Bible study. If you need help with a practical approach to sharing the saving message, I'd suggest my book, *Eternal Life, Believe To Be Alive.*

57
FRUIT ABUNDANT FRUIT

Sweet news spreads the fastest. After years of waiting, your joint effort with Lenard's family has paid off. All of the work has now resulted in a massive crop of the sweetest fruit you've ever tasted. It turns out that Loola was right. With the first basketful of fruit, you are already looking for people to share with.

"Hey, Beth and I were thinking we could pass out some fruit," Lenard says one Saturday morning. Beth holds a large basket at her waist which is filled to overflowing.

"Pass it out to who?" you ask as you pluck sweet handfuls to fill your own.

"Well, we have way more than we could ever eat or even preserve," Beth explains. "We could give some to the neighbors."

"Give *some*," Lenard says to Beth. "We could give tons to the neighbors and still have too much." It doesn't take any more convincing. You're in, as long as Lenard and Beth are there.

You spend the morning going door to door with your

baskets of fruit. It doesn't take long to empty the baskets. Your neighbors are overjoyed to have fresh fruit. You're walking back toward your house with Lenard and Beth after all the fruit has been disbursed.

"Did you notice how many people said they wanted to grow a fruit tree?" you ask.

"The Johnsons," Beth offers.

"Eric too," you say.

"Didn't Linda say she wanted to plant a garden as well?" Lenard asks.

"Wouldn't it be cool to start a garden club?" you say. "Think how many different kinds of fruit we could have in the neighborhood."

"Not to mention, getting to know everyone better. I mean, it was gardening that brought us together," Beth says.

Over the next few weeks, you make more fruit deliveries to your neighbors. You bring up the idea of starting a garden club with Eric, Linda, and the Johnsons. They all respond with enthusiasm but insist that they don't have a green thumb. Lenard shows off his human-colored thumbs and wins them over each in turn.

Lenard offers to help Eric start his garden. Beth makes friends with Linda, and they do the same. You offer to help the Johnsons get their portion of the orchard started, and they accept.

Over the following years, the neighborhood changes in the sweetest ways possible. More fences come down; more fruit trees go up. The Johnsons share their newfound passion with Gary. Gossiping Gary complains a bit, but even he plants a tree. It rarely bears much fruit, but at least he gets to be in the garden club. Eric and Linda spread the excitement to others as well. With every season, calling the joined backyards *the orchard,* is less and less ironic.

After many years have passed, you find yourself standing in the shade of the fruit tree. You think back to that seminal moment when you dropped that seed into the wild earth. It feels like a lifetime ago, and it was. So much has changed, but one thing has remained. Your ultimate purpose, your grand gardening goal. You have always been:

IN PURSUIT OF FRUIT.

THANK YOU

Thank you for reading In Pursuit Of Fruit. Please come and visit our website and see what me and the team are up to at WWW.FREEGRACE.IN

If you enjoyed this book, please leave an honest review where you bought it, it helps us get our message out to as many people as possible.

ALSO BY LUCAS KITCHEN

NON-FICTION • Naked Grace • Things Above • Eternal Life: Believe To Be Alive • Salvation and Discipleship: Is There A Difference? • Eternal Rewards: It Will Pay To Obey

CHILDREN'S BOOKS • Good Enough • Evan Wants To Go To Heaven • Adventures Beyond Mudville

NOVELS • For The Sake Of The King • Cloud Haven • Below The Huber Ice

For a list of all of Lucas' books, visit **LUCASKITCHEN.COM**

END NOTES

2. YOU THE JUNGLE

1. This book is written to those who have already believed in Jesus for eternal salvation. If you've yet to believe, I'd suggest reading my book Eternal Life: Believe To Be Alive.

4. ABUNDANT DEATH

1. Which includes a soul and spirit.
2. Luke 8:14
3. Galatians 6:19-21 ERV
4. Romans 8:6
5. 1 John 3:9
6. Romans 7:22 MSG
7. Romans 8:7
8. Romans 8:6 CSB

6. THE GOAL OF YOUR LIFE

1. John 10:10
2. Romans 7:4 CSB
3. Galatians 5:22-23

8. GOD WANTS ABUNDANCE

1. John 10:10
2. John 13:35 NIV
3. If you would like to know more about the difference between salvation and discipleship, I've written a book on the subject. It's called Salvation and Discipleship: Is There A Difference?
4. Psalms 16:5, 73:26, 142:5, 119:57, Lamentations 3:24
5. If you would like to know more about eternal reward, I've written a book on the subject called Eternal Rewards: It Will Pay To Obey
6. Hebrews 11:6

10. TRANSFORMATION

1. Romans 7:7-8, 15
2. Romans 12:1 NKJV
3. I Corinthians 3:16

12. MINDSET

1. Romans 12:2
2. Colossians 3:2
3. Colossians 3:1
4. Reward is not eternal salvation, but a repayment for a believer's obedience.
5. Philippians 4:6-9 (edited for brevity)
6. Isaiah 26:3
7. Philippians 3:19
8. Colossians 2:18
9. 2 Timothy 3:7-9

14. WHY IT WORKS

1. Philippians 4:6-9 (edited for brevity)
2. Romans 8:5
3. Romans 8:11

18. NO FRUIT NO ROOT

1. Eternal Life: Believe To Be Alive
2. John 6:47
3. John 10:28

20. DON'T FORGET

1. Romans 7:10 NIV
2. Romans 7:24

22. DON'T SWAP

1. Romans 8:6 CSB
2. Matthew 23:27
3. Matthew 6:4, 6:6, 6:18
4. Galatians 5:19-26

24. ESCAPE ARTISTS

1. John 5:36
2. Mark 16:20
3. 2 Timothy 3:12 CSB
4. John 16:33 NIV
5. John 12:42-43 CSB
6. Romans 1:18
7. Revelation 3:19
8. Romans 5:3-4 ESV
9. James 1:2-4 CSB
10. 1 Peter 1:6-7 CSB

26. ROTTEN FRUIT TEACHERS

1. 2 Peter 3:14-16
2. 2 Timothy 2:2 CSB
3. Matthew 7:15-20
4. Matthew 12:33-34
5. Acts 17:11 CSB
6. Matthew 7:22
7. Matthew 7:23

28. TRY HARDER

1. Matthew 10:38-42

30. CULTIVATING SIN

1. Luke 8:7
2. Luke 8:14
3. Hebrews 12:1

4. James 1:15 NIV
5. Hebrews 3:13
6. Romans 8:15-24

34. WHY PRAY

1. Philippians 4:6-8
2. 1 Thessalonians 5:17
3. Romans 8:26-27
4. Matthew 6:5-6

36. BEGINNER'S GUIDE TO PRAYER

1. Matthew 6:5-6
2. Matthew 6:7-8
3. Matthew 6:11
4. Romans 8:26-27
5. Matthew 11:30
6. Galatians 5:22-23

38. TRANSFORMED BY CONFESSION

1. Matthew 6:12
2. Romans 8:7-8 NLT
3. 1 John 1:9
4. 1 John 1:7
5. 1 John 1:6, 8

40. REQUEST TRANSFORMATION

1. Matthew 6:13
2. Romans 8:13 NKJV
3. Romans 8:11
4. 1 Corinthians 10:13
5. Matthew 5:28
6. Lyrics from Lashes on the 2010 release, Yet, from My Epic.
7. Romans 8:13 NKJV
8. Romans 12:2
9. 2 Timothy 2:22

42. YOUR OWN BIBLE

1. John 21:22-23

44. WHY STUDY

1. Acts 2:42
2. 1 Peter 2:2 CSB
3. Hebrews 4:12 ERV/NKJV
4. Colossians 3:16
5. Hebrews 5:10-12 CSB
6. Luke 24:24
7. Psalm 119:169
8. James 1:5 NIV

46. BIBLE BOREDOM

1. Luke 11:28
2. Psalm 119:16, 25, 28, 50, 81, 107,147, 162
3. Psalm 119:103
4. Acts 2:42
5. Colossians 3:16 NKJV
6. Colossians 3:16 NKJV
7. My favorite word-for-word Bible songs are written by Ross King. He's put out a project called Every Last Word. You can find it on any of the streaming services, or wherever you buy digital music.

48. TRANSFORMED BY SCRIPTURE

1. Psalm 119:11 ESV
2. 2 Timothy 3:8
3. 2 Timothy 3:16-18
4. Colossians 1:10 NKJV
5. 2 Corinthians 3:18

50. ABUNDANCE IN FELLOWSHIP

1. Hebrews 10:24-25
2. Galatians 5:22

3. 1 John 4:7
4. 1 John 1:3-4
5. Philippians 2:2
6. Matthew 18:20

52. FELLOWSHIP BY SERVICE

1. Acts 2:42
2. Acts 4:32
3. Galatians 6:10
4. Galatians 5:13
5. 1 John 3:11
6. Romans 12:6-8
7. Romans 12:9-13

54. TRANSFORMED BY FELLOWSHIP

1. Galatians 5:13
2. Hebrews 10:24-25 ESV
3. Hebrews 3:13 CSB
4. James 5:19-20 CSB
5. Proverbs 18:1

56. BRINGING OTHERS IN

1. Matthew 5:15-16
2. John 13:35
3. Romans 15:7
4. Matthew 28:19-20
5. For more on this topic see my book Salvation and Discipleship: Is There A Difference?
6. 1 Peter 3:15
7. 2 Timothy 4:5